CONQUEST

THE ALFURIAN CHRONICLES
BOOK 3

AARON HODGES

Proofread by Sara Houston
Illustration by Eva Urbanikova

ABOUT THE AUTHOR

Aaron Hodges was born in 1989 in the small town of Whakatane, New Zealand. He studied for five years at the University of Auckland, completing a Bachelors of Science in Biology and Geography, and a Masters of Environmental Engineering. After working as an environmental consultant for two years, he grew tired of office work and decided to quit his job in 2014 and see the world. One year later, he published his first novel - Stormwielder.

FOLLOW AARON HODGES...

And receive TWO FREE novels and a short story!

https://aaronhodgesauthor.com/newsletter

ALSO BY AARON HODGES

The Sword of Light

Book 1: Stormwielder

Book 2: Firestorm

Book 3: Soul Blade

The Legend of the Gods

Book 1: Oathbreaker

Book 2: Shield of Winter

Book 3: Dawn of War

The Knights of Alana

Book 1: Daughter of Fate

Book 2: Queen of Vengeance

Book 3: Crown of Chaos

The Evolution Gene

Book 1: Reborn

Book 2: Havoc

Book 3: Carnage

Descendants of the Fall

Book 1: Warbringer

Book 2: Wrath of the Forgotten

Book 3: Age of Gods

Book 4: Dreams of Fury

The Alfurian Chronicles

Book 1: Defiant

Book 2: Guardian

Book 3: Conquest

The Swords of Heaven and Hell

Book 1: Darkstrider

The Four Circles

Book 1: Help! My Wizard Mentor Had A Heart Attack And Now I'm Being Chased By A Horde Of Giant Spiders!

The Untamed Isles

The Path Awakens

PROLOGUE

Serena Levaanton, Alfurian Princess of the planet Talamh, knelt in the darkness. Stones dug into her skin through the threadbare pants she wore. Whenever she shifted position, her ankles screamed in pain, the heavy shackles that bound her slicing into her flesh. She had long since ceased to notice the stench of her own body, though dirt and grime covered her normally translucent skin from head to foot.

A roar erupted overhead, sending a shudder down her spine. The crowd. The humans were celebrating, glorying in the success of their champion. Egging him on—cheering for the death of their ancient foe.

For the death of one of her brothers.

She hadn't seen who it was. That was the first thing she'd learnt, these last six months. Not to look. Or listen. Or care for anyone but herself, and her silent companion in the darkness.

Her father, former Prince of Talamh, Elder of her people.

Shivering in the chill of their cell, Serena clenched her fist. Even six months on, the absence of her Manus reader —the device that allowed her to manipulate Light—still stung. That had been the first thing the human invaders had done, after the conquest. Rounding up her people, they had been surprised at first by the devices. But surprise had turned to anger when they'd learned their purpose. The Manus readers had been torn from every one of the Alfur they'd captured. An agonising process, given the devices had been surgically implanted into their palms in adolescence.

Of course, the device would not help Serena now. They had long since starved her of the Light she needed to fight. The power of the universe no longer flowed in her veins, no longer granted her its strength. The humans that had come from the stars knew better than to feed an Alfur. They had been ancient enemies once, but those days were long since past.

Humanity had won, apparently,

Now they ruled the galaxy, while the Alfur—her brethren—had been condemned to servitude.

Everywhere, but for precious, hidden Talamh.

The golden planet, its surface lush with jungle and wilderness, its oceans untouched. It had remained protected for centuries from the human Federation, hidden away by the force known as the Haze.

Until a group of local humans had discovered its source, and destroyed it.

Fool that she had been, Serena herself had led them to it.

She hadn't known any of this, of course. Her father and the other Elders had fooled them all—the humans of Talamh and the Alfur both—telling them tales of Alfurian conquest and supremacy.

Until six months ago, Serena had believed her father and the Elders the cruel ones. Afterall, they had ruled over the humans of Talamh with an iron fist for centuries. So it was in the spirit of hope that she had led a rebellion against her father. She had thought to find another way, to bring human and Alfur together in mutual respect, so they might finally find a way to work together.

Fool.

How could she have been so naïve?

Instead of peace, the human, Hazel, had smashed the machinery of the Haze and sent a distress signal out into the universe. The Federation hadn't taken long to respond. Unprepared, the Alfurian defences were crushed by Federation ships before they'd even known they were under attack. Serena and her father had been captured with the rest of their people in Goma. Rumours swirled in those first few weeks, that other cities might have resisted, that a few might have escaped the indomitable forces of the human Federation. But in the end, they were only rumours. None could stand against the might of the Federation.

And then had come the first games.

Death matches between gladiators had long been a tradition of the humans of Talamh. The Elders had encouraged them, in fact, thinking the games an acceptable outlet for the innate aggression of humanity.

But the Federation had seen an opportunity in the games. An opportunity to punish their ancient enemy.

Somewhere overhead, the crowd cheered again. This time the noise continued, like the roar of a distant storm. Serena's heart sank. So the Alfur had fallen. She wondered if it was one of theirs—an Alfur born of Talamh, and freedom—or if it was one of those the Federation had brought to the planet.

That change had started more recently, when new Alfur had appeared in their neighbouring cells. At first, she'd thought them Alfur from other cities, captured at last after months on the run. The truth was crueller still. The newcomers did not from Talamh at all, but other planets. They were Alfur deemed too much trouble to keep as slaves, sent now to Talamh to fight and die in the games.

Chains rattled as Serena shifted, clenching her fist again around the scar in her palm, frustrated by her weakness. For all the years her people had lived on Talamh, her father had dreamt of the day others might join them here. That he might find a way of rescuing the of their people and bringing them to safety.

Now finally they would see the open skies of Talamh. But not for liberation. They would find only death here, death at the end of a burning blade of Light.

Fool, fool, fool!

Serena exhaled as the roar of the crowd began to subside. They would come for them soon. In the darkness, she sensed her father stir. His overly large eyes appeared as he woke.

"Is it time?"

Serena clenched her fist. "Remember, stay behind me."

A flickering light appeared as she spoke. Or rather, Light, as an attendant moved down the corridor outside their cell, carrying a platter set with two glasses. Her blood stirred at the sight of the Light within each. This would be the only meal they received all month—just before they were to battle to the death. She supposed it wouldn't make much of a show otherwise, if they fought while starving.

She tried not to appear too eager when the attendant paused outside and waited for the buzz that would unlock their cell. When it came, he pushed open the door and set the platter on the ground before them. He backed up quickly, as though fearful they might launch themselves at him. Small chance of that, weak as they currently were. But the humans of Talamh had spent their entire lives viewing the Alfur as a deadly threat. Old habits were slow to fade.

Once outside and with the doors closed again, the human took a device from his pocket. A few presses of its buttons and the door clanged, the locks resetting. He lingered a moment, waiting to see what they would do with the Light. Neither Serena nor Aiden moved from their seats. They still had *some* dignity, little as it was.

The caretaker seemed to realise this, as with another press of his remote, the shackles on their wrists and ankles clicked open and fell to the ground. He gave a snort of derision—funny how they were always brave *outside* the cage—and retreated down the corridor.

Serena rose slowly, rubbing at her chafed wrists. Her entire being trembled with hunger, and her legs shook as she stepped over to the tray and lifted the glasses. Mostly, she and her father spent their days in an almost trancelike state, a type of hibernation that let them survive the month between games without losing their minds to the hunger.

She could feel her weakness as she sank back to the bench beside her father. It took all her strength to set the second glass down for him, rather than take it herself.

"You should...drink it." He rasped in the gloom.

Serena shuddered at the strength that must have taken, to offer up his own meal. She longed to do as he said. Instead, she took her own glass and downed it in a single gulp. It was a moment before her body began to process the sudden offering—then she gasped as power surged through her limbs. Within seconds, every muscle and sinew was set aflame, tingling with renewed energy. Even the world seemed different, the darkness of the dungeon more...vibrant.

Only then did she have the strength to incline her head and reject her father's offer. "You need it as much as I do, Father," she whispered. "Without it..."

She couldn't finish, though they both knew the truth. Aiden Levaanton was centuries old. His body was worn, and without regular Light to preserve him, he was withering away by the day. He wouldn't survive another month without sustenance.

Though if she failed above, neither of them would survive the next hour.

A shudder ran through the ground beneath their feet. Serena exhaled as the floor began to lift. So the time had come. She looked at her father, then his glass of Light.

"Take it, Father."

Her twin hearts pounded hard in her chest as she waited for him to obey. Bit by bit, the bars to their cell disappeared as they were lifted into the shaft above the cell. The Light in the glass seemed to grow brighter as the stone walls enclosed them on all sides. Until, somewhere overhead, the ceiling shifted and sunlight streamed down on them.

A lump lodged in her throat as her father was revealed by its glow. Like her, grime covered him from head to foot. But where she now shone with the fresh Light pumping through her system, his skin was a paled, wrinkled grey, his eyes so sunken that his face appeared more skull than flesh.

Again she clenched her fist around the absent Manus reader. But there was no fight to be found there. Instead, she took the glass and pushed it into his limp hand. He looked at her then, and she saw the despair in his eyes, the doom that had grown month after month in this terrible captivity.

"You need it more than I, Daughter."

"No, Father," she replied with steel in her voice. "We survive together, or not at all." She closed his fingers around the glass. "So drink, and then let us see which humans they have sent against us this month."

Aiden Levaanton stared at his daughter for a moment longer, but his gaze no longer carried the weight of the man who had ruled over Goma for generations, and finally he acquiesced. Serena watched in relief as he swallowed the Light and some life returned to his face. Not much, not enough, but it would have to do.

Then the daylight swallowed them up. It was all Serena could do to keep from closing her eyes against its brilliance. Squinting, she cast her gaze around the arena. Humans packed the stands, already on their feet and jeering at the sight of their former rulers. They had all learned to know their local Alfur by sight over the past months. Given their history, Serena had no doubt she and her father were the most despised of all those who appeared at the monthly games.

A pity for them that she had so far proven a match for every gladiator they had sent against them. But then, unlike the rest of her people, she had fought in this arena, even before the conquest. For years she had fought under the moniker of Rotin, defeating every human who had challenged her. Much as she might regret those days of bloodlust, if it hadn't been for that practice, she and her father would have fallen months ago.

As it was, Serena Levaanton drew in a breath of humid jungle air and stepped from the platform onto the sands of the arena. Her boots were so thin by now she felt their heat through the leather, but she didn't hesitate. She strode forward to the twin blades plunged into the ground and tore them loose. Despite the grim spectacle she was about to participate in, Serena immediately felt better with their weight in her hands. Now, win or lose, at least she would not die on her knees.

The jeering of the crowd had died down somewhat now, as their eyes turned towards the opposite side of the arena. Serena followed their gaze, while behind her, Aiden Levaanton retreated to the shadows. He was no coward, but her father had little combat experience. They both knew he would be a liability if he tried to help in the coming fight.

Movement came from the sands as the stairwell to the human partition of the arena opened. They would send two against her, she knew. Off-world humans, most likely, men or women who had committed crimes against the Federation and been condemned. Not soldiers, thankfully, nor the professional gladiators that had graced these sands under Alfurian rule. That had saved her, these last six months. For while the prisoners she fought now might be untrained, they did possess Light.

And that alone was enough to make them deadly.

Frowning, Serena focused on her own core, on the

Light pumping through her veins, infusing her body. It thrummed with the music of the strange blue sky overhead. The sky that had changed on the day of the conquest. With the fall of the Haze, the emerald glow she had known all her life had faded to this sapphire blue.

Yet another reminder of her failure...

Swallowing her regret, Serena fixed her eyes on the pair of shadows that emerged from the stairwell. Two men, one older, his hair a stark silver, the other young with a matted beard. They marched onto the shining sands to the soft boom of drums. She didn't move. Not yet. An almost invisible barrier stretched across the arena between them, separating the combatants. It would fall when the drums reached a crescendo.

Instead, she began to stretch, flowing through a series of exercises she had perfected in her days as Rotin, the Alfurian gladiator. With all the time spent in the cramped cell beneath the stadium, her body needed to be loosened. For a brief moment, she allowed her eyes to close, allowed herself to savour the warmth of the sun on her skin, the freshness of the air. If not for the impending danger of battle, she might have looked to these days with anticipation.

She came to a stop as the drums sped up, turning towards her opponents. One of the men—the younger— was already stalking up and down the barrier, a weapon of pure Light in his hands. Unlike the Alfur, humans could manipulate Light without a conduit, and so preferred to use Light weapons to the more traditional blades she held.

Ordinarily, they would cut through the steel of her blades with barely a flicker of resistance, but Serena had learned months ago how to feed her own Light into the weapons, reinforcing them. She did so now, even as her gaze was drawn to the older of her foes.

This one hadn't moved, hadn't even summoned a weapon. He stood with his arms crossed, his steely gaze fixed straight ahead. Her hands tightened around the hilts of her swords. Where the first seemed angry, perhaps reckless, this man...this man she couldn't read. Hopefully his age would slow him.

The beat of the drums was almost one now, the roar of the crowd all but deafening. Serena sought out her Light. The man that stalked the barrier practically shone with the Light he was burning, but she kept the flow to her own limbs at a trickle, enough to add speed and power to her movements. She would never match the brute strength of humans, with their ability to create Light. But she could match them with speed and grace of Alfurian movement.

Abruptly, the drums all around the arena fell silent.

The barrier flickered and died.

The young human exploded across the sands towards her.

And Serena Levaanton, Alfurian Princess of Talamh, met him blade to blade.

ONE

IT WASN'T THE SCREAMS THAT BOTHERED JOHANAS.
Or at least, not the most. Nor was it the sight of the terrible wounds suffered by the gladiators—though those were bad enough. It wasn't even the pointlessness of it all. The knowledge that hard as he might try to save these sorry lives, in another month, both human and Alfur would be sent back onto the sands, to fight and wound and die all over again.

No. It was that he couldn't use his Light.

After a lifetime of feeling powerless, he had finally discovered the brilliance within himself—only to have it constrained by order of the Federation. While every human possessed some degree of destructive power, most struggled to do much else with their Light. Johanas was one of the few capable of more, of using his power to heal.

Except here in the arena infirmary.

According to the Federation, these men and women were not worthy of such an ability. Condemned by intergalactic laws Johanas was barely beginning to comprehend, the Federation would have rather let them to bleed out and die, than see them treated at all.

That much, at least, Johanas would not stand for.

A seemingly random jumble of words came from the young Alfur on the table as he struggled to stem the bleeding from the wound in her stomach. Her eyes were scrunched closed and he imagined she was pleading to some unknown god from her planet—based on the multitude of scars crisscrossing her pale skin, she had not enjoyed the luxurious lifestyle of the Talamh Alfur. There were few enough of those left at this point, so most of the Alfur he treated now came from off-planet.

Lifting his cloth from the wound, Johanas checked the bleeding. Seeing the flow had slowed to a trickle, he set aside the rag and took up his needle and thread. Concentrating on the needle point, he gathered a spark of the Light that now burned in his core, and allowed it to flow over the steel, sterilising it.

At his use of Light, the Alfur's eyes snapped open. Their silver glint was dull, starved, but at the sight of his power, her lips moved and this time he understood the words.

"Light...just a little...please..."

Johanas swallowed as she began to sob. He knew even a little would help to save her—over the past months, he'd grown to appreciate the Alfurian people's skill with the Light in a way he never had before the Haze had fallen. He'd had plenty of chances as a gladiator to witness the Alfur using their Light, before their Manus readers had been torn from them. When he used his power, he wielded it like a sledgehammer, healing wounds through sheer force of will. But for them...

For the Alfur, the Light was something entirely different. They used it like a jeweller with precious gold wire, crafting it with care and precision, working miracles on the barest flicker of power.

He longed to fulfil her wishes. A spark would help her with the pain and stave off infection...but one of the guards was watching. So instead he could only grimace and give a shake of his head.

It stung, to see the despair in her eyes, the tears on her translucent cheeks, but he forced himself to concentrate on the needle and thread, and doing his best to stitch the poor Alfur back together. He couldn't have said how long he stayed like that, working amidst the dim backlight of the arena infirmary, fingers intent on the delicate work. Only that by the time he finished, his patient had grown still, passed out from the pain.

Stepping back, he looked down at the unconscious girl. She was tiny, this Alfur. Much smaller than average. They aged differently to humans, with much of their development dependent on access to Light, so it was impossible to tell her exact maturity, but he had a feeling she might be a teenager by Alfurian standards. He wondered what distant world she had come from, what one so young might have done to be so condemned by the Federation as to be sent here.

His stomach twisted. Her breathing was shallow, ragged. It was a terrible wound, and he had no idea how she'd defeated her opponent in the arena after she'd taken it. Not that her survival would earn her much of a respite. Resilient as the Alfur were in general, not even they could heal from this in under a month—at least without Light. And if she didn't recover in time for the next games, she would likely be put in one of the group bouts, where a half dozen Alfur were thrown into the ring without weapons to be hunted by a pack of wild beasts.

It was...barbaric.

They were barbaric, his people. He used to think it was the Alfur that made them like this—and later the Haze. Only now did he understand how wrong he'd been.

Another scream snapped Johanas back to the present. There were others who needed his attention, and the games still continued upstairs. He wondered if this would be the month that Serena Levaanton and her father finally fell. The streets of Goma had been buzzing this week about the match. There was talk of the Queen bringing in a pair of real fighters to face them.

Johanas had tried not to listen to the rumours, but it was hard to ignore the guilt that weighed on his shoulders for Serena's fate. And, well, this Alfurian girl, she reminded him of the one who might be fighting for her life even now, of the only Alfur on Talamh that had ever given a damn about the humans they governed.

He cast another glance in the direction of the guards. No one was looking now. Quickly he reached out and allowed a flicker of Light to pass from his fingers to the girl. She stirred, eyes flickering beneath her eyelids, but did not wake. Hopefully she would put it to good use. He could offer her no more without risking the glow seeping from her skin.

He moved away before anyone noticed his extra attention, and found Jasmine Holt already attending the next patient in the line of makeshift beds.

Johanas had found him on the first day of the conquest, not long after the sky had turned from green to blue and the Federation ships had descended upon the city. She hadn't said much in those first days, but when she'd seen the wounded he'd been helping to heal in the streets, she had immediately moved to join him.

It was only later that he'd realised who she was. Jasmine Holt, former leader of the resistance, traitor of humanity. Everyone thought she had died all those months ago, when she'd turned against her own people. So for the most part she'd gone unnoticed in those early days. But Johanas had recognised her. The resemblance to his friend Rydian—her son—was too great to ignore.

It had been weeks before he'd gotten the full story from her, about what had happened in the soaring towers of the Alfur, how the world had been so changed. He and Falcon, the gladiator champion of Goma, had been the distraction on that day, starting an uprising in the middle of the city and drawing the Alfur's attention.

The distraction had worked, allowing Rydian and fellow gladiator Hazel to infiltrate the tower of the Alfurian prince. But he had heard nothing more from them.

So it had fallen to Jasmine to tell the tale. Of how Rydian and Hazel had found her in the tower, of how she had begged them to turn back, and how they had refused. Of how the Alfurian Prince, Aiden Levaanton, had come, and how by the pleas of his daughter, he had finally shown them the truth.

That the Alfur were not galactic conquerors, but refugees who had fled from the human Federation.

How they and the humans that came with them had created the Haze to hide this planet.

And how that creation had become a double-edged sword that drove the Light-imbued creatures of Talamh insane.

The Alfur had given Manus readers to humanity at first to protect them from the Haze.

But in doing so, the humans of Talamh had also been cut off from their own Light. From the very power that allowed them to stand as equals with the Alfur.

And finally, she had told Johanas how Rydian had collapsed, succumbing to the effects of the Haze. How the Alfur had been ready to kill him, before Hazel had destroyed their machinery controlling the Haze, and sent a distress call out into the galaxy, pleading for help.

So Talamh had fallen.

And Jasmine Holt would never forgive herself for the part she'd played in its conquest.

Which, Johanas supposed, made them much alike in that regard. He too had blood on his hands from that day.

So here they worked, tending to the doomed, doing what little they could to fix what they'd helped to break.

She looked up as he approached, offering a nod before returning her gaze to the Alfur she was helping. This one was male and in better condition than the girl he'd just mended. His arm hung loose at his side, its flesh purpled and broken in several places, as though it had been struck repeatedly by a heavy weapon. The patient twisted and turned as Jasmine tried to set the bones straight.

"Johanas," she growled, gesturing in frustration, "hold him still."

He did as he was told, placing one hand on the Alfur's chest and the other on the Alfur's good arm. The overly large, silver eyes fixed on him with a terrible intensity and its lips drew back into a snarl.

"Relax," Johanas snapped as he felt the creature pressing against him. He fed Light to his muscles to rein-force them against the wiry Alfurian strength. "We're here to help."

The Alfur didn't seem to believe him and continued to strain, while Jasmine did her best to set the shattered bones. Thankfully, the Alfur must have used most of its Light in the arena and was no match for Johanas's strength.

Finally Jasmine grunted, apparently satisfied it was as

straight as it was going to get, then turned to fetch the materials for a cast.

Johanas found himself staring at the translucent skin of the Alfur's broken arm as he waited. If he looked hard enough, he could make out a few of the fractures in the bone beneath. He shuddered. It wasn't life threatening, but without Light, this too would take longer than the month the Alfur had to recover.

Before he could think about what he was doing, Johanas again allowed his Light to flow into the Alfur. His patient's eyes widened with shock. Thankfully, the offering finally seemed to convince the creature of his intentions, for it sagged back against the bench. He grimaced, eyes flickering around the room, but Jasmine returned before he could see whether any of the guards had noticed.

With the Alfur no longer struggling against them, it took only a few minutes to bandage up the limb. But when they made to move away, the patient finally spoke.

"Why?" he rasped, confusion showing in his silver eyes. "Why help us?"

Jasmine did not look back, but Johanas hesitated. "Because it's the right thing to do."

A roar came from overhead, making a lie of his words. The ceiling shook as the crowd came to their feet.

"I..." the Alfur's eyes were distant. "I will have to fight again?"

"You have a month to recover."

The Alfur's head fell, but when he said no more, Johanas moved after Jasmine.

"You know you're not supposed to give them Light," she muttered when they were out of earshot.

His head jerked up. "You saw that?"

"I'm not as blind as the simpletons they send to watch us."

He sighed, then shrugged. "What are they going to do?"

"Throw you into the arena with the rest of their human prisoners?"

Johanas snorted. "Not likely. The people remember..."

He didn't finish. Of course the people remembered. He had bathed Goma in blood the day he'd lead the uprising. He just wished *he* could forget.

"For now, Johanas," Jasmine murmured, "but we are a vicious race, with short memories. Do not expect their gratitude to protect you forever."

She moved away, skirting the next bed, which contained an injured human, and moving towards the next Alfurian casualty. He sighed. Jasmine refused to go near human patients these days. Johanas was about the only human she wanted anything to do with. She hadn't even allowed her Manus reader to be removed. Unlike just about every other human on Talamh, Jasmine Holt remained cut off from the Light.

Johanas thought about that as he looked over the injured human. Would it have been different if Rydian had survived?

Was that at the heart of all her bitterness—that she had allowed Hazel to destroy the Haze in a desperate bid to save her son, only to have it fail? That had taken the longest to get out of her. How she had run to his side as the Haze collapsed around them, holding him tight, begging him to stay...

...only for him to fade away, for his breath to stop, his body to go limp.

The Federation hadn't even let her bury him. They had found them in that room, drawn by the signal Hazel had broadcast. Aiden and Serena Levaanton had surrendered without a fight when the human soldiers came through the door. They had taken everyone in the room into custody. Jasmine and Hazel had been released a few hours later. But Rydian's body...no one knew what had been done with him.

That hurt for Johanas, not getting to say goodbye, to look one last time at the friend who had fought for him, who had saved him. What must it be like for Jasmine then, to know she had sacrificed everything she believed in, only to find it all for naught?

The man only had a few cuts and scrapes—though unfortunately this didn't improve his demeanour. He complained the whole time Johanas spent looking over him about being placed in the same room as the 'stinking Alfur'. That seemed to be a common attitude amongst the human prisoners sent to Talamh. They might be criminals, but at least they were *human* criminals. The Alfur were little better than beasts as far as they were concerned.

Having witnessed the technological genius of the

Alfur for most of his life, it was an attitude Johanas couldn't understand, but he had long since given up trying to convince these humans of their error. In the end, human or Alfur, if they had been sent to Talamh, their destiny waited on the end of a sword. No one else had been allowed to visit their backwater planet yet—or at least, no one but the first soldiers that had come, and a few high-level officers who had visited to make an assessment of the society.

When he finished with the human, he joined Jasmine working on the next Alfur. This one had lost her arm in combat. Thankfully she was unconscious, allowing them to work undisturbed. Not even the Alfur could regrow a limb—as far as Johanas was aware—so the best they could do was stem the bleeding and bandage the wound.

Another roar came from overhead as they finished, and this time Johanas couldn't keep his eyes from drifting to the ceiling. Were those cheers for Serena's opponent? Were the rumours true, and the day had finally come where she would fall?

"Forget her."

Johanas started at Jasmine's words. "Who?"

"The Princess. She's doomed, she and Aiden. Doesn't matter whether it's today, or next month, or six months from now. There's nothing either of us can do to save her. You'd best accept it."

With that she turned and walked away. There were no more Alfur to treat just now, and she disappeared through the doorway that led to the mess hall. Johanas's stomach twisted as he watched her go. He wanted to argue, but what more was there to say?

Strange. They were on the winning side this time.

So why did it feel like they had lost, all those months ago?

TWO

Energy crackled and sparked as Serena's blade met the human's weapon, turning aside the burning Light that would have torn through her ribcage and cooked her from the inside out. Teeth bared, she spun on her heel, delivering a riposte of her own that forced the human to hurl himself back to avoid a beheading.

Serena used the opening it brought to cast a glance at the second human. The older man still hadn't moved. That was something at least, since the younger of the pair was proving a difficult enough opponent as it was. She would have struggled to protect herself and her father from both. Of course, she didn't know *why* the human had chosen to forgo their numerical advantage, but this didn't seem the time to question it.

Another wicked slash of her opponent's blade brought her attention back to the battle. The man was stronger than her, of that there was no doubt. His dark skin practically *burned* with the Light he was giving off and his weapon was constantly changing shape, making it difficult for her to anticipate one attack from the next.

Just now, he had settled on a longsword, and its greater reach to Serena's gladius had forced her on the defensive. That was fine. With the Light burning in her veins, she had all the energy she needed to turn aside his blows—and wait for her opening.

It would come eventually, she knew. It always did with this kind of fighter. Confident in their own innate power, they would hammer away at her defences all day, thinking themselves invincible. That there was no way an Alfur could possibly harm them.

Five times now, she had shown the arrogant humans of the Federation the error of such thoughts.

Maybe on the sixth, they would finally learn.

With each clash of their blades, sparks flashed and the crowd cheered. They loved to watch her being beaten back, to witness their former overlords humbled. And who could blame them?

Serena caught a vicious blow on the edge of her sword, but such was the power behind the human's swing that she was sent lurching backwards. The stadium shook as the spectators came to their feet, roaring their approval. She was quick to disappoint them, recovering and bringing her sword up to defend the next blow.

It didn't come, as instead she found the man grinning at her from across the sands.

"Never killed a princess before," he laughed, gesturing

at her with his shining blade. "Those golden eyes will make a pretty souvenir."

"Why don't you come and take them then, pretty boy?" Serena sneered. "I've seen teenagers with more skill than you."

"Fancy words, for an Alfur," the human growled. "We'll see if you sing to the same tune when my blade is buried in your belly!"

With a roar, he hurled himself at Serena again, his blade of Light swelling as he raised it in a two handed grip above his head, forming a massive butterfly headed axe.

Perfect.

Strength rushed to Serena's muscles as the Light she'd been holding back swept through her body, bursting from her skin in a sudden brilliance. Sand exploded behind her as she surged forward. A flicker of panic appeared in her foe's eyes, a sudden realisation. She took a small measure of satisfaction from that.

He had overdrawn his weapon, preparing for a blow that would have torn her in two. But that blow would never fall, as Serena drove her short sword through the man's belly, angling it up beneath the ribs in search of his heart. That was the best way to deal with these Light imbued humans, she'd found. They tended to shrug off even the most serious of wounds otherwise, their innate Light either allowing them to ignore the pain or stem the bleeding. But a blade cleaved through the heart...

The massive axe vanished in a puff of Light as the human sagged against her. Breath hissed softly from his lungs and the glow of Light died in his eyes—even as blood pumped from the wound, covering her weapon and hands.

Wrinkling her nose, Serena twisted her blade, allowing the body to slide sideways and fall to the sand. She stood there a moment, puffing gently in the humid air, staring down at the body. Another victory. But it was only half done.

She drew the Light thrumming in her channels back to her core—that second heart pumping away in her chest—and looked for her next foe.

He was still watching her, those strange eyes finding her from across the stadium. He hadn't moved the entire time—but now a smile touched his lips as their eyes met. Without a word, he started towards her.

Serena fell into a fighting stance, sword extended—though the man had yet to summon a weapon of his own.

"Stay back!"

Her opponent didn't respond, only continued his path forward. Sand crunched beneath his boots as he made his calm way across the stadium. Serena hesitated, unsure what was happening. Why hadn't this man fought with the other against her, like her previous bouts? Why only move now the second human was dead?

All around the arena, the crowd had grown silent, expectant. Did they know something she didn't? They *really* wanted to see her and her father dead, but...they seemed just as confused as Serena as to the second human's actions.

"I'm going to give you one last warning," she hissed, pointing her sword at the man's throat.

Still no response. Serena cursed beneath her breath. Why was she hesitating? It wasn't like they would let them walk away from this fight without further bloodshed anyway. The humans she fought were prisoners as well— just the more regular criminal sort. If they didn't fight, someone higher up would intervene to punish them. She couldn't risk them throwing her and her father to the wolves.

Her grip tightened around the hilt of her sword as Serena made up her mind, and with a growl she sprang—

Whomp!

The breath hissed between Serena's teeth as Light flashed from the man, coalescing into a blast that swept aside her sword and slammed into her chest. If it had formed a blade, or been stronger, she would have been as dead as the man she'd just faced. Instead, all it did was hurl her several yards across the stadium.

Slumped on the ground, Serena wheezed, struggling to regain her breath. The crunch of footsteps on sand continued. Clenching her teeth, she pushed herself to her knees and searched for her sword. Finding it nearby, she scooped it back up and swung around, preparing for the next attack.

But her foe wasn't coming for her—he was moving towards her father.

No!

Imbuing precious Light into her gladius, she charged

across the sands. A glow lit the blade, which finally seemed to draw the man's attention. His eyes flickered in her direction as she closed with him. The Light emerged from his body again, but this time Serena was ready. Her blade hissed out to meet the blast, slicing through the burning white, thrusting towards her foe...

Clang!

A spear of Light materialised in the man's hand, blocking her attack before it could tear out his throat. She leapt back, expecting a riposte, but the man did not advance. A smile touched his lips.

"She has your fire, Aiden."

Serena's blood ran cold. How...how did this man know her father's name? From the corner of her eye, she saw her father's head jerk up, saw his eyes widen and his lips part to whisper—

Then the human was upon her.

This wasn't like her first foe.

There was no fury here. No emotion. He came at her with a cold inevitability. The butt of his shining spear smashed into her blade once, twice, a third time. Each time, the power behind the attack was...overwhelming. On the fourth, not even the Light she had infused into the fragile metal could save it.

Her gladius shattered into a thousand pieces.

Serena staggered back as a wave of pain swept through her body, as though she had been the one to take each of those strikes. The human towered over her, still advancing, that slight smirk twisting his thin lips.

Shaking her head, Serena threw off the pain and clenched her fist around the hilt of her shattered blade. She could sense her father watching them, sense his fear as the man spoke again.

"A shame, Aiden. Had she been born human, I would have said she showed promise. But alas, she will always be limited by the deficiencies of your race."

Anger gave Serena strength. Perhaps this man was not so different from the others after all. Too bad. Let his arrogance be his undoing. The spear faded away as he approached, and she saw her opportunity. With a roar, she lunged, driving the jagged piece of steel that was all that remained of her blade at his exposed throat.

The human moved. A simple twist of his body, a flick of his hand, a push of his foot, and she lay sprawled in the sand, the sword hilt tumbling from her grip. She gasped, but even as the pain of her landing caught up with her, she struggled to push herself back up, to scramble for her lost weapon—

A heavy boot slammed down on her back, driving her face first into the sand.

"I must say, it was a pleasure to learn you had a daughter, Aiden," the man's voice whispered.

Spitting sand from her mouth, Serena fed what remained of her Light to her starving muscles and surged back up. To her relief, the pressure vanished from her back and she rolled sideways, scooping up the sword hilt and swinging in the direction of her enemy.

He wasn't there.

A whisper came from behind her. "I've been waiting for this day a long time."

Serena gasped as icy pain exploded through her abdomen. Her eyes fell to her stomach, where a blade of Light had pierced her through. A tremor shook her as she stared at the deadly weapon. Agony wrapped about her, setting her every nerve on fire, but she found she couldn't scream, couldn't even move. A heavy hand settled on her shoulder. She tried to resist, but her strength failed. She sank to her knees. The arena...seemed eerily silent, even as she heard her father screaming, somewhere in the distance. She wondered...wondered what had become of the crowd.

The fire vanished as the blade was yanked back. Serena swayed where she knelt, but the hand on her shoulder would not let her fall. Her eyes were still on her stomach. It seemed so small, the wound. Barely a thumb wide. Her shocked mind struggled, like her thoughts were wading through sludge. She'd survived injuries worse than this before. When she had Light to draw on...

"Saxon Colley."

Serena flinched. Her father's voice...he was close. He shouldn't be so close to this human. He was dangerous. He would kill the old Alfurian prince without any effort at all...

"I did not think to find anyone left, after all this time."

"You thought I would forget?"

A shove from behind sent her crumpling forward, but to her surprise, warm arms embraced Serena before she could fall. Stars danced across her vision as she looked up into her father's eyes.

"No," she whispered, struggling to speak through the pain. "Run...Father."

"Where would I run, Daughter?" he said with a sad smile.

Serena slumped against him, her entire body trembling. How could the human move so fast? She'd never seen anyone fight like that...except, maybe, *Rydian*? Had he moved that fast?

"All this time, you thought you could escape. But the Federation remembers, Aiden. You should have known that better than most."

Serena shivered. The Federation? So...this was no prisoner, no criminal, but an actual Federation soldier. She swallowed, looking into her father's golden eyes. They were fixed on their foe, but his hand was resting on her shoulder, and she felt the trickle of Light as he let some of his power flow into her.

He wanted her to use it to heal, she knew, but what good was that if they remained trapped with this man. Clenching the flickering glow within, she sent it to her muscles instead, and forced down the pain.

Then she pushed off her father and turned, placing herself between the pair.

"Stay back," Serena snarled. "I won't let you hurt my father."

Their enemy chuckled. "Truly she is loyal, Aiden. Surprising, for the daughter of a blood sucking leech." The humour slowly drained from his face as he watched them. "But if she will not stand aside..."

"Saxon, no—"

Her father didn't get to finish as the man launched himself forward. Serena tried to react, tried to burn enough Light to match him, but in her injured, exhausted state, it wasn't even a contest. He battered aside her clumsy blows and caught her by the throat. She tried to scream as he hauled her into the air, but fingers like iron cut off her voice. Stars burst across her vision as she clawed at him, trying to prise his hand loose. Darkness swirled but she fought against it.

"Please, Colley, spare her. Take me instead!"

"Oh I will, Aiden," her foe hissed. "Eventually. But first, I want you to feel the pain I felt. To watch as someone you love dies in front of your eyes."

Light flickered in Serena's fading vision. A burning sword appeared in the man's hands. She gasped, too weak now to even struggle. Her Light, even the Light her father had lent her, was exhausted, and her body had nothing left to give.

All she could do was watch as her opponent raised his blade for the final blow.

THREE

RYDIAN HOLT, FORMER GLADIATOR OF GOMA AND saviour of the planet Talamh—at least as far as the Federation were concerned—stood at the enormous window of the star ship and stared into the cosmos. Beyond the Lights of the ship, the universe was dark, the distant stars mere pinpricks against the endless black. It made him shiver, thinking of all that emptiness, of the void between worlds.

Though he knew it was not the void he should fear, but the pinpricks. Each represented another world, another planet conquered by the ever-expanding Federation. They stretched across the galaxy, hundreds upon hundreds, worlds of sand and endless water, lush forests and cities that filled entire worlds. Each inhabited by a different species. Each ruled by humanity, governed by their Lightmakers.

Rydian found himself shivering. If even a whisper of his plans were to reach them...

He shook himself, carefully schooling his thoughts. While abilities with the Light varied wildly between individuals and species, it was not unheard of for a skilled Lightmaker to pluck whispers from another's mind.

Exhaling, he forced himself to calm. He had covered his tracks well, these last months. No small achievement, given he'd awoken on a planet that was not his own, with an individual that was neither human nor Alfur leaning over him, four eyes staring out of a purple face.

An Androculus, humanity called them. Though few remained of their species, they specialised in healing Light and little else. Small surprise they had lived beneath the regimes of one galaxy conquering species or another for all of known history.

Apparently, the human soldiers that had responded to Hazel's distress signal had found him near death in the chamber beneath the Alfurian tower. Reading his Light signatures, they'd mistaken him for someone important and delivered him to the best healing facility in the galaxy. They had brought him back from the brink, apparently.

They had also taken him from Talamh, the only world he'd ever known.

Once, the thought might have excited him. Afterall, he'd spent half his life dreaming of the stars, of the infinite possibilities they represented, that one day a saviour might descend to free the beleaguered humans of Talamh.

Now though, the absence of home left a hollow feeling in his stomach. For while the stars had indeed offered salvation, it was not the kind he had expected.

Wherever the Federation went, wherever they ruled, the Alfur suffered. Those who had governed Rydian's entire life, he found now crushed and broken, bowed beneath the weight of servitude. The Federation barely viewed them as living things, let alone equals. They were tools to be used, servants to be punished, playthings to be discarded.

Even a year ago, Rydian would have enjoyed the sight of his former overlords so humbled. But that was before he'd lost his hand and discovered the Light within him. Before he'd met Serena Levaanton. Before she'd saved his life. Before she'd help the humans of Talamh stand against her own people. Her own father.

Balling the fingers of Light that had replaced his severed hand into a fist, Rydian prayed he was not too late. With a shiver, he turned his gaze from the vast depths of space and looked towards their destination.

Talamh.

His home world stretched out before their ship, a great globe of blue ocean and green forests, stark mountains and endless yellow grasslands. It looked so small from here, so delicate, like he could reach out and encompass everything he'd ever known in the palm of his hand. Like it could be crushed with a thought.

That was probably how the Federation viewed it.

They'd been wary, he knew, when they learned what had happened on the planet. That somehow, a population of Alfur had escaped their notice. That generations of humanity had been cowed and broken, enslaved as they themselves had enslaved the Alfur across the galaxy.

Such an event went against the natural order of things, as far as the Federation was concerned. Rydian had even heard whispers that they'd been close to cleansing the planet, just to ensure the corrosion couldn't spread. He might have thought such rumours an exaggeration, if he hadn't spent the last few months learning their past.

The Federation soldiers might have overestimated Rydian's importance on Talamh, but their monitors had not been wrong about his abilities. The capabilities of every human varied with age and practice, but Rydian was apparently somewhat of an enigma. Once he'd woken and the top brass of the Federation had learned about his abilities, they'd been eager to initiate him into their training systems—even if Talamh remained quarantined from the rest of the galaxy.

So it was that he'd spent the past few months learning the true nature of his power. Without the Haze constantly threatening to tear his mind to shreds, the training had proven surprisingly easy. His progression had even surprised the tutors at the academy. Within weeks he had surpassed the other first year trainees. A month, and even the second years were lagging behind him.

At six months, he'd learned everything the academy could teach, and shattered the record for earliest graduation.

Which was just as well, since Rydian had no intention of lingering longer. He was needed elsewhere. Even the

Federation seemed to agree with that, given that several generals had made competing offers for his inclusion in their forces. Apparently not even conquering the known galaxy was enough for humanity. New soldiers were needed as they explored new frontiers and tamed the wilds of broken worlds.

Thankfully, Rydian's performance in the academy had earned him some lenience, and in the end he'd been allowed a brief hiatus to reconnect with his home.

Rydian could only hope it would be enough.

"How long until we land?" he asked, turning from the window and approaching the man who stood at the bridge.

"We're engaging the landing process now, sir."

Rydian nodded. Apparently, his graduation from the academy made him an official member of the Federation military, and therefore of a higher rank than any civilian. Even though he hadn't even officially 'signed up' or fought for them yet. It seemed a strange system to Rydian, but then he was from a backwater planet that hadn't even been on the map until a few months ago, so what would he know?

"Shouldn't be more than an hour now until we touch down," the captain continued. "You know, for a non-Federation planet, this Talamh place has some interesting technology. You see those towers? They're transmitting a Landing Guidance Telemetry that'll bring us right in on the central structure. Never seen anything like it. It's a shame we're not allowed to interact with the general population yet. I would love to ask about the architect who built those things."

"The Alfur created them," Rydian said absently. That was probably information he was technically meant to keep reserved, but what did he care?

The captain didn't take him serious anyway. "The Alfur? Right, good one, sir."

Rydian ignored the comment. He'd learned pretty quickly that no good could come from arguing on behalf of the Alfur. At best, people thought them unintelligent beasts, good only for menial labour. They would certainly never believe the creatures might have a culture or society of their own.

"You must have impressed some people in high places to be granted a visa to visit this place," the captain continued conversationally as he worked the controls.

"Something about breaking a graduation record," Rydian grunted.

His eyes were on the planet surface again. The path of the ship had brought the city of Goma into view. His city. The first thing you saw were the Alfurian towers the captain had mentioned. Great, soaring masterpieces of architecture, they had loomed over his entire life, seemingly stretching forever for the stars.

But those were not his home. His home, the city of his birth, lay in their shadows, in the sprawling slums of lower Goma. There, building upon building covered every inch of ground, their spread confined only by the enormous walls that guarded against the maddened beasts of the jungle outside.

Though, Rydian saw now this was no longer the case. Only six months had passed since the Haze had fallen, freeing the animals of Talamh from their madness, but already some enterprising humans had ventured outside the walls and begun to build.

"Must have been some performance," the captain remarked. "If it convinced the brass to wave the quarantine for you. What inspired you to choose this planet anyway?"

"I was born here."

"Wait...really? But..."

"The Federation only discovered us six months ago. Doesn't mean we didn't exist before that."

"Right..." the man trailed off. He seemed suddenly nervous and kept glancing in Rydian's direction, as though just now realising he'd invited a barbarian onto his ship. "So, ah, *how* exactly did you go undiscovered for all those years? Seems like you had the technology to say hello at least." He gestured at the distant towers.

Because our ancestors created a device that destroyed all Lightmakers and trapped us on the planet, he wanted to say.

He kept his silence instead. He'd already said too much. The Federation might be eager to learn what they could from the Alfurian technology on Talamh, but they were just as eager to keep word of its source to themselves.

Afterall, they wouldn't want Alfur in the rest of the galaxy to learn of their brethren's successes. They might get ideas.

His stomach twisted at the thought of those he had seen suffering beneath the reign of the Federation. Alfur beaten and broken, men and women and children, born and raised and dying in slavery, so that all they ever knew was servitude. Even the average human in the streets seemed little better off than his own people on Talamh, toiling away as they did, without a hope of ever lifting themselves up from the muck.

And now...now he would turn his back on all of them. He knew in his heart there was nothing he could do to change this universe, to crush a system as enormous as the Federation. Rydian might be unusually gifted in the Light, but he was by no means the only one. There were soldiers within the Federation army with decades of experience, men and women with so much accumulated power they could have crushed him with a flick of their hand.

No, the universe was the Federations to conquer.

But not Talamh. Not if he had a say in the matter.

Exhaling, Rydian closed his eyes and reached for his newly honed powers. Before, whenever he'd touched his Light, a thousand voices had erupted in his skull, screaming their torment. Now...now the Light around Talamh was undisturbed by the Haze. He could still hear the voices, but now they were whispers, like a million tiny bees buzzing below him.

They came from other animals, other species connected to the Light. He wondered what had happened to them after the Haze was disabled, whether anything had been left of their minds. Fatimah, the giant cat he had bonded, had been close to madness when they'd found one another.

They had left her on Talamh when they'd taken Rydian, so he reached for her now. To his joy, he sensed a flicker of recognition in the city, followed by the warmth of her touch upon his consciousness. He smiled, sending reassurance through their bond, before his senses expanded to find Johanas and his mother nearby. Neither sensed his approach, but he still sighed with relief. They were alive—and together. Thank the gods below. Now if—

Rydian froze. What was *that*? That...presence...who...

His eyes widened.

And with a crackling of Light, Rydian vanished from the bridge of the starship.

FOUR

SERENA SCREAMED AS THE BLADE OF LIGHT descended, thrusting out a hand, though of course her frail flesh would do nothing to prevent the blow from landing.

Boom!

An explosion of Light slammed into the ground between Serena and her foe. Sand lashed her face as the force of the blast picked her up and sent her tumbling backwards across the ground. Agony shot through her abdomen as she landed. A scream tore from her lips and it took all her strength to cling to consciousness. She hadn't seen what had happened, only that it hadn't come from the human.

Coughing, she struggled to open her eyes, fearful of the brilliance, but the Light had faded as quickly as it had appeared. Blinking away the stars in her eyes, she managed to lift herself onto her elbows. Her father stood nearby, eyes wide with surprise as he stared at the swirling vortex of dust that had erupted from the centre of the stadium.

Blood thrummed in Serena's ears as a silhouette appeared amidst the cloud. It shifted, head moving as though in search of something, before a burst of Light thrust the dust away, clearing the air...

...and revealing the face of a young man.

Serena's hearts stilled as his sapphire gaze swept the stadium and settled on her.

Rydian.

Where had *he* come from? What had happened to Colley...

...she had the answer to that question at least as the dust cleared, revealing a crumpled body on the far side of the arena. She held her breath, waiting for the man to move, but whatever Rydian had done, Colley didn't seem in a hurry to get back up.

Her gaze drifted to the crowd of humans. A heavy silence hung over the stadium now, as a thousand eyes peered down at them, trying to make sense of the newcomer that shone so brightly with Light.

A lump rose in Serena's throat as she turned back to the Goman gladiator. The crowd were waiting to see what would happen next.

Rydian Holt.

Last she'd seen him, Serena had stood over his helpless body with sword poised to strike him down. Was that why his gaze was so intent, why his eyes burned as he watched her. Had he returned for vengeance? If so, he was months too late for that. Serena had lost everything since the conquest. All she had left now was her life.

And her father.

"Rydian Holt." Her father's voice was soft as he spoke. "I wondered if it was you that I sensed."

Rydian's eyes flickered. "Aiden Levaanton." His voice was colder than it had been before, deeper. His gaze took in her father for a moment, before shifting in the direction of the unconscious fighter. "Friend of yours?"

Serena's hearts were still racing. That look in Rydian's eyes, was it anger? She couldn't tell. Human emotions were...confusing. She couldn't let him hurt her father. He was all she had left. A groan slipped from her lips as she tried to stand, the pain momentarily overwhelming her self-control.

"Serena."

She flinched. Suddenly Rydian was standing over her, his forehead creased in a frown. She couldn't help but think of the reversal this represented to the last time they'd seen one another, when she'd steeled herself to strike him down. She braced herself for the hiss of Light that would come when he summoned a weapon.

Instead, he offered her a hand. "You okay?"

Ha? She stared at the extended digit for a long moment. "Uh..."

"You look...hungry. Here." His skin began to glow as he reached down and touched her shoulder.

Hunger didn't begin to describe Serena's state—

The thought was swept from her mind as a *surge* of

Light flooded from Rydian's hand into her body. Not scraps. Not even a little glass of the stuff, but a venerable *flood* of power. Her secondary heart truly began to race now as the brilliance surged through her Light channels, setting her every nerve aflame and restoring her strength, pressing back the pain.

By the time Rydian withdrew his hand, her body was already putting the newfound power to work. Fibres of Light swept through her abdomen as she closed her eyes, directing the energy to her damaged flesh, helping to mend the torn fibres back together. In seconds she had restored what would have taken days to repair, weeks even. The damage was bad enough that it couldn't be healed immediately, but with the amount of power Rydian had given her, months of healing could be achieved in mere hours. A miracle, truly.

And *very much* against the rules.

Her eyes snapped open as the first rumblings of discontent began amidst their audience. They were starting to suspect the figure in Light was not there to take vengeance against their former rulers.

Rydian didn't seem to care.

"Are you alright? Was that too much?"

Serena struggled just to open her mouth to reply. Her body *burnt* with the power he'd given her, her channels shining through her transparent skin for all the world to see. She couldn't understand why he had done it. She hadn't missed the gold diamond badge on Rydian's chest. The Federation soldiers had worn them the day they'd conquered Goma. He was one of them. And yet...

"Yes," she whispered at last. Gathering the energy she could spare from her wound, she pushed herself to her feet. Only then did she hesitate, glancing in the direction of her father. It was pushing this unexpected luck, but... "Could I share it with him...sir?"

A frown creased Rydian's forehead and for a second Serena thought she'd said the wrong thing. Then he followed her gaze and saw her father lingering nearby. Without a word he marched across to where Aiden Levaanton stood and laid a hand on his shoulder.

A second later, the Light channels all over her father's body lit up like a meteor shower. The rumbles of discontent from the crowd rose to jeers as they realised what he'd done for the two of them. Serena felt only relief as she stumbled across the shifting sands and embraced her father. He hugged her back, and for the first time in months, there was real strength in his arms.

When they separated, Rydian was still there, but the crowd was really growing boisterous now. Hazel wondered why no one had intervened. Only moments had passed, but...where was the Queen, with all her cruelty and hatred—

"I understand we have been enemies in the past." Rydian's voice drew her back to the human standing between them. He extended his hand to her father. "But I think it's time that enmity came to an end."

Her father stared at the offered digit for a long

moment before looking into Rydian's eyes. "Your own kind might have some objections," he replied at last.

A wry smile was Rydian's only answer. The hand remained, and eventually her father reached out and took it. Serena kept her eyes on the crowd. They were really growing rowdy now. Most were on their feet by and hurling abuse down at those on the sands. She hadn't seen them like this since the conquest. It was only a matter of time before words turned to violence.

"Don't suppose you had a plan to appease that lot then?" she asked.

"Yeah, I ah, didn't think anyone would be stupid enough to keep this tradition going," Rydian muttered darkly. "Who's in charge here these days anyway?"

Serena stared at him. Could he truly not know? She still couldn't trust what was happening, *why* it was happening. By all rights, Rydian should be here to kill the both of them. There was a part of her that still believed she deserved it, after what she'd done. After what her own people, her own father, had done to humanity on Talamh. What they'd done to their own allies...

"Serena? Are you alright?"

She started, and found Rydian still watching her. It was definitely concern in his eyes now. Did she really look that lost? Though...something had changed in the stadium while she'd been lost in her thoughts. It took her a moment to realise what it was.

Silence.

A tingling spread through her skin as she looked at the

crowd. They were still on their feet, but their eyes were elsewhere now, their voices quelled.

"You're about to meet her," she said, choosing to answer Rydian's original question. She wasn't sure whether she could answer the second.

Are you alright?

She had spent six months starving, locked away in the darkness, her only glimpse of sun or Light on the day she was forced to fight for her life.

Rydian had noticed the crowd now as well. She watched as he swung around, looking for the reason for the silence. A lump lodged in her throat and her hearts thrummed to the oscillations of her Light. He really didn't know.

"Rydian..." she began, before another voice boomed across the arena. A familiar voice.

"Rydian Holt!" They spun to find a figure garbed in gold marching across the sands towards them. "I should have known. You always did like to flirt with disaster."

FIVE

TRANSPORT TO THE SURFACE OF TALAMH HAD LEFT Rydian nauseous and slightly disorientated. He'd only used the ability a few times in training, and then only over short distances. But what he'd sensed from the arena, Serena's pain, the boiling hatred of the crowd...there'd been no time to spare.

And he'd barely arrived in time. The human Serena had been fighting was powerful. In his panic, Rydian had hit him with just about everything he had. Yet he could still sense the Light swirling around the unconscious gladiator. He would have a splitting headache when he woke, but the man was far from finished.

Then there was the reaction of Serena and her father to his appearance. Serena might be from an entirely different species, but there was no mistaking the fear in her eyes when he'd appeared. The pair looked like they half expected him to take over the fight for the fallen gladiator. Serena at least had trusted him before. Didn't she remember they were allies?

And now there was a familiar voice, shouting out his name.

"Rydian Holt! I should have known. You always did like to flirt with disaster."

He spun, heart leaping in his chest as he glimpsed the face of his friend.

Hazel.

She strode across the sand towards him, ash blonde hair bouncing in the sunlight. She was wearing a long, flowing dress of golden fibres. Of all the various outfits he'd seen her wear as a gladiator, this had to be the strangest of all. But there was no time to comment on her attire as she came to a stop and glared up at him with those familiar brown eyes.

"Hazel," he said with a smile. "I'm so glad to see—"

"It's Queen Hawk now," she interrupted.

"Ah..." Belatedly, Rydian noticed the golden circlet nesting amidst her long locks of hair. He'd been so distracted by the fact she was wearing a *dress* that he hadn't spotted it. "Wait..." There was a full second where he processed that information. "You're...joking, right?"

Hazel's face darkened. She hadn't exactly been known for her mellow personality as a gladiator. At least that much was the same.

"A lot has changed since you left us, Rydian," she replied, her voice like ice. "Though if the report I read last night is true, you should at least know not to give Light to these…beasts." Her eyes flickered in the direction of Serena and her father.

Ice spread through Rydian's veins at her words. Pursing his lips, he looked down at the young woman before him, at the friend that had fought by his side to free Talamh from the Alfur. Or at least, that was what they'd *thought* they were doing. Just like him she'd hated the Alfur then, having lived her entire life beneath their rule. But…surely she could see times had changed, that it was not the Alfur, but the Federation that threatened to crush all hope of freedom from their planet.

Unless…perhaps this was only a façade she put on before their audience. He hoped so. The crowd was already beginning to rumble again. He could sense the ripples of their emotion on the air, their anger at being denied vengeance against the two Alfur.

"What's the matter, Rydian?" Hazel continued when a minute had passed without him saying anything. "Did you lose your tongue galivanting around on your adventures off-world?

"My off-world…Hazel, where do you think I've been these past months?"

The crowd were finding their voice again. Apparently not even an appearance by their queen—*Queen*—was enough to keep their anger contained. Rydian sensed movement behind him as Serena and Aiden shifted closer to him.

Hazel noticed as well. "I see you've reacquainted yourself with our former Overlords." Her eyes narrowed.

"Now if you're quite done, you'd best stand aside so General Colley can finish with his playthings."

"*General* Colley?" Damn, that was bad. He tried to keep his eyes from drifting in the direction of the man he'd downed. Maybe he *should* have hit him harder.

"Yes," Hazel said slowly, as though she were speaking to an idiot. "The man you attacked. Here I was thinking that badge on your chest meant you'd learned a bit of discipline."

Rydian could only stare. This...this Hazel was not the woman he remembered, the friend who had fought at his side. What had happened while he'd been away? His gaze flickered at another roar from the crowd. A man had tried to climb over the barrier separating them from the sands, but guards had tackled and restrained him.

"I don't understand what's happening here," he said. "Why is the arena still operating? Why are gladiators still giving their lives on these cursed sands? After everything we went through, I would have thought you of all people would have torn this place down."

"You *would* think that." She wandered past Rydian, until she was face to face with Serena. To Rydian's surprise, the Alfur shrank back from the queen. The cool, calm Alfurian warrior he'd known before the conquest would never have retreated so easily. "But where would the justice be in that?" Hazel continued. "They had our people bleed on these sands for generations. It only seems fair for their reign would end in the same way."

Rydian looked at the body lying on the sand nearby.

Not the general he'd knocked down, but another that Serena had apparently killed before his arrival.

"And yet our people still bleed."

"Rogues and criminals."

"They said that about us, not so long ago."

"Enough!" Hazel snapped. She took on a haughty tone. "You speak of matters you do not understand, Rydian Holt. If you wanted a say in the governing of Talamh, you should have stayed, instead of abandoning us."

Rydian said nothing. In that moment, he had glimpsed the pain in his friend's eyes. The hurt.

"The Hazel I knew railed against slave masters," he murmured. "She would never have become one."

"Hazel died the day your mother murdered my brother," she hissed. "The day *they* put me in chains and threw me into the arena to kill or be killed. Now there is only Queen Hawk. And I won't stop until every last one of our former tormentors are dead."

"If that's true, then I am truly sorry," Rydian murmured, bowing his head.

"I don't need your sorries, Rydian. I need you to get out of my way."

"Then I am afraid I must apologize a second time. You can't have them."

"Is that so?" Hazel sneered. She made a gesture over her shoulder. "And what exactly do you plan to say to your superior officer when he wakes? He paid good money to make sure those two died today."

Rydian crossed his arms. "Did he now?" He flicked a glance to where the man lay still. "Funny, I didn't see a badge. If I had to guess, I'd say this wasn't an official visit."

Hazel's face darkened, but he continued before she could speak.

"In which case, that makes me as the highest-ranking Federation official on Talamh."

"I am queen—"

"And I came back to help my friends," Rydian continued. "If you no longer count amongst their number, I suggest you stay out of my way...Queen Hawk."

Hazel didn't reply this time, only stood seething on the golden stands as Rydian turned from her and approached the pair of Alfur.

"In my capacity as a private of Federation Armed Forces, I am requisitioning these two Alfur," he said over his shoulder. "If you—or any other civilian on this planet— have a complaint, you may send that by official communication to high command. From what I've heard, you should expect a reply in a week or three."

"Don't do this, Rydian." Something in Hazel's voice froze Rydian in his tracks. He glanced back, and for a second he saw the mask slip, glimpsed the fear in her eyes. "Don't fight this war. You won't win."

A lump rose in Rydian's throat as he matched eyes with his friend. Or former friend? They had fought together on these sands, trained together, celebrated their victories and mourned the loss of friends. It seemed impossible he would march into this battle without her. But...

"I'm sorry, Hazel," he whispered. "You haven't seen what I have, these last six months. I can't just close my eyes to it all. You know that."

They stayed like that a moment longer, gazes locked. Hazel was the first to break away, her eyes flicking to the stands. The crowd were on their feet and jeering, but their roars had faded into the background for Rydian.

"I know, Rydian." The words were so softly spoken that he hardly heard them. And when Hazel's gaze returned to his, he saw not anger or hatred there, but sadness. "I know."

He swallowed, but there was nothing left to say now, no turning back. With a final nod, he turned and placed a hand on Serena and Aiden's shoulders, and drew them into the Light.

SIX

THE MECHANICAL DOORS TO HAZEL'S CHAMBERS opened with a gentle hiss as she approached, the sensors responding to her personal Light signature. She strode inside without a backwards glance, then sent a burst of Light at the panel on the other side to close it. A high-pitched whining came from the doors as they slid back into place. She'd used too much force, but in that moment, Hazel hardly cared.

This day...gods below, this day had been a nightmare. Damn the Alfur. Damn Rydian. Damn the stinking Federation and their goddamn general. Not that he was meant to even be here. Rydian was right about that much. The bribery it must have taken, even for someone with such a high rank...well, Talamh was still adopting the Federation credits system—which was just as well, since their old currency had been tracked on their Manus readers—so she wasn't exactly clear on the value of what he'd given her *personally*. But it had to be a small fortune.

She'd been curious, of course, when he'd contacted her. After all, this was a man who commanded battles across entire solar systems. What could motivate someone with that much power to lower himself so far as to face an Alfur in single combat. It wasn't exactly a position anyone else in the galaxy was lining up to fill.

Despite her curiosity, she would probably still have denied him. The Federation had been clear that only authorised off-worlders were allowed on the planet surface. The last thing she wanted was to anger their leaders enough that they revised their initial decision over Talamh's fate. She'd heard enough from the soldiers they'd sent in those first days to realise...other options had been discussed. It chilled her to think how close they might have come to planetary annihilation.

Ultimately though, that was the same reason she had acceded to the general's demands. Stuck between a wall and an Alfurian blaster, she'd chosen the most prominent threat.

Which had been all well and good, until Rydian goddamn Holt had decided to ruin everything.

Grating her teeth, she stomped across the room and flopped down on the leather sofa in the middle of her chambers. Gods, never mind the general—Rydian's little stunt had just about started a riot in the middle of Goma. Again. That was the kind of chaos she was meant to be preventing.

Three people had died before her guards had dispersed the crowd. A disaster, though only a fraction of what it could have been, had things gotten further out of hand. The riot had been bad when they'd overthrown the Alfur. Now most humans in the city had removed their Manus readers and had access to Light...

The Federation should just be grateful that Hazel had handled it with minimum bloodshed.

But of course, she would get no thanks from them.

And that had only been the beginnings of the crap storm Rydian had left in his wake.

Her next task was dealing with the Federation general.

At least Rydian hadn't killed the man. Having to explain to the Federation how one of their top commanders had died on her planet—let alone what he was doing there in the first place—would have probably been the end of her and Talamh both.

Not that her position was much better with him still breathing. She'd spent the last few hours apologising to the man, and begging him not to launch an assault against the visitor's tower in which Rydian had taken up residence. That was yet another blow to her authority. She'd had that tower prepared and staffed for the day the first true ambassadors of the Federation visited the planet.

Instead, the Federation had gone behind her back and arranged for it to host Rydian's little visit.

Hell, they could have at least warned her earlier that he was returning!

Hazel lay her head back against the cushions and

stared at the ceiling. She wanted to rage and scream and hurl something breakable against the wall. Why was this happening? The fall of the Alfur was meant to make everything right. Instead, Hazel felt as though she were walking a tightrope across a canyon, where a single gust of wind would plunge her and all of Talamh into the abyss.

And Rydian Holt was a goddamn hurricane.

In the end, she'd convinced the general to stay his hand, if only to avoid further scrutiny by the Federation. Two Alfurian prisoners cut down in combat might have passed under the radar, but a battle between two Light-makers—and powerful ones at that—in the skies above Goma? Yeah, that would probably be noticed.

But the man was far from happy with the outcome. He would have his vengeance, one way or another.

So as always, it was up to Hazel to resolve the situation.

Groaning, she twisted on the couch, trying to get comfortable—but the damn dress she still wore made that all but impossible. It was too long for her liking, and the way it hugged her body was very impractical in terms of movement. If she ever needed to fight in one of these things, her opponents would fall over laughing watching her tripping on the thing.

Truth be told, she'd rather be wearing her armour.

Unfortunately, the Federation was a big fan of appearances. She needed to accustom herself to these outfits if Talamh was ever to be opened to the galaxy.

Although that didn't mean it was needed in her private chambers.

She was halfway through undressing when the tap came on her door. She clenched her teeth. It didn't take much to guess who *that* would be at this time of night. She was in no mood for company, but Falcon wasn't the sort to go away easily. Slipping on her dressing gown, Hazel sent a burst of Light to open the door. She deliberately overcharged it this time, so that the doors squealed as they opened.

"What do you want?" she snapped as the woman on the other side was revealed.

Falcon's face was screwed up in pain from the harsh sound. Served her right. Rather than answer Hazel's question, the former champion of Goma shook off her discomfort and laughed. She strode past Hazel before the other could stop her.

"Falcon," she snarled as the woman dropped onto the sofa. "I am *not* in the mood for your antics."

"Oh my, someone's in a tizzy today, aren't they?" Lying back in the cushions, the woman arched an eyebrow. "Aren't you going to offer your visitor a drink?"

"*Uninvited* visitor. And no, not until you explain why you're here."

The woman snorted. Reaching into her leather jacket, she drew out a flask and shook it with a smile. "I guess I'll play the part of host then." She took a swig, sighed, then held it out for Hazel.

She eyed it a moment, before rolling her eyes and

snatching it from her friend's hands. The spirits burned as they went down, and she came back up spluttering.

"Gah, that's truly terrible."

"Tastes like home," Falcon replied with a grin.

Hazel snorted. Crossing to the corner where she kept her own store of various liquors imported from across Talamh, she took down a pair of glasses and poured them each a glass of cognac. She returned to the sofa with one in each hand, only to pause, holding the glasses tantalisingly out of reach of the former champion.

"Talk," she demanded.

"Oh, fine," Falcon replied with a roll of her eyes. "A little birdy told me you were having a bad day."

Hazel said nothing. Nor did she hand over the glass. Falcon would have to do better than that if she wanted it.

"Well? Oh don't be such a bossy boo...fine! If you want details, I saw the broadcast from today. Rydian's back. Didn't look like you two were getting along either. Figured you might want to talk." She lay back on the sofa, arms spread out on either side and a lazy smile on her lips. "So... do you?"

"Not really," Hazel muttered.

She handed over the cognac anyway. Falcon raised it in reply and they chinked glasses.

"To comrades past and present," she murmured.

Hazel's insides twisted, but she said the words anyway, then sank onto the sofa alongside her friend. Nothing was said for a time, as they each sipped at their drinks, minds lost in silent thought.

"What am I going to do?" Hazel said at last. "Hell, what is *he* going to do."

"We both know the answer to that second one."

Hazel nodded. "Something rash."

"Question is, are you going to join him?"

"*Join* him? Why would I join him? He's siding with the enemy!"

"Girl, the Alfur aren't our enemy. At least, not anymore," Falcon replied, her voice strangely calm. "Even were the Federation to leave today, the Alfur could never rule us like they did before—not now that we have our Light." Falcon's hands began to glow at her words. There was a hunger in the woman's eyes as they lingered on that power.

Hazel downed her glass. Rising, she crossed to the liquor cabinet and returned with the bottle.

"They will *always* be my enemy," she whispered.

"But not Rydian's."

"I don't want to talk about Rydian!" Hazel snapped. "Six months!" She gestured wildly at nothing in particular. "Six months I've been working to placate the Federation and in one day he burned up every iota of progress I've made."

Letting out a sigh, Falcon crossed her legs. "And doesn't that tell you something?"

"Tell me what, Falcon? That I'm all alone? That my friends would rather work against me than help make this world a better place?"

"Johanas never left, Hazel—"

"Don't call me that!" she snapped. She drew in a harsh breath to calm herself. "And he may as well have. He chose *her*, didn't he?"

Silence. Then...

"I don't agree with what Jasmine did to your brother," Falcon said softly. "But times have changed. We all have blood on our hands now, Hazel."

"The only blood on *my* hands is from the guilty."

"Oh yes," Falcon sneered. Now she came to her feet as well. Snatching up the cognac she drank a swig straight from the bottle. "Perfect, powerful, Queen Hawk could *never* make a mistake. That's why we're positively *surrounded* by friends here, right?" She burst into laughter, the sound harsh in Hazel's ears.

That was it. Hazel lashed out without thinking, hurling her half empty glass at the gladiator's face. But Falcon hadn't become champion for nothing, and she snatched the crystal vessel from the air with ease.

"My, my," she tisked. "Temper...my queen. Someone might think you...were still affected by the Haze." She took another swig from the bottle and swayed on her feet. Her eyes had already taken on a distant look. "Well, I can see... you're in a particularly...bitchy mood today. So my job is done! I'll leave you... to stew in your own...misery. Kisses!"

Turning, she staggered across to the door. Hazel could only shake her head in pity for the woman's state. This was how every night ended. The former champion showing up at her door. Some brief conversation, before Falcon got her hands on the bottle. Then...

...then she was gone, leaving Hazel alone. And despite the fire of their fights, despite the unpleasantness of her friend's state, somehow every night Hazel felt worse after the champion left.

Because she knew no one else would come.

She was all alone.

SEVEN

THE ARENA VANISHED.

Serena opened her mouth to scream as the world dissolved in a flash of white—only to suddenly find herself in a sleek corridor of steel and glass and...

...she stared out the enormous window in front of her. At the familiar view stretching out below, of the sprawling mass of Goma, of the verdant jungles all around. It was a view she seen every day of her life, prior to the conquest. Only the sky had changed—instead of the shimmering emerald, now a clear blue sky stretched across the planet, all the way to the distant curve of the horizon.

Home.

This was their tower, the tower of her family, the seat from which her father had ruled Goma for centuries. Why had Rydian brought them here?

"Sir!"

The yelp of a man behind Serena had her jumping on

the spot. Light sprang to her hands as she spun, though without a weapon or Manus reader, it could do little more than reinforce her physical body. Thankfully it wasn't necessary, as she found herself standing in front of a very surprised looking man in a tightfitting suit not unlike what the Alfurian pilots had worn. He stood staring at the three of them for a full second longer, before his mind finally seemed to click into action.

"Ah, sorry, sir," he stammered, saluting. "You, ah, startled me. What can I do for you?"

"The apologies are all mine, captain." Rydian seemed slightly disorientated himself. "I wasn't sure quite where else to direct us. I figured you might know where I was meant to be staying during my visit."

"Oh, yes, of course..." the man said quickly. "After your...abrupt departure from my ship, I brought us in to dock as per my instructions from the Federation. This tower has been designated as accommodation for foreign dignitaries and distinguished guests from off-world," he paused, "which at this moment appears to be just you, sir."

Rydian blinked. "So...you're saying I have an *entire tower* to myself?"

"It would appear that way." A sudden grin broke across the man's face. "Hey, what do you think, maybe I'll get to meet the architect that created these towers after all."

Serena frowned. What was this man talking about? Rydian seemed distracted as well. He kept glancing out the window, as though he still wasn't sure whether they might be followed.

"Sure, captain. I'll see if Aiden here wants to chat with you later," he said absently. "For now, I'd be obliged if you could find us a few empty rooms to shower and rest."

"Ah...did you...umm, yes, I believe there are a few off-world retainers somewhere who have been assigned as caretakers. Let me just..." the captain trailed off as he pulled a tablet from his pocket and began fiddling with its screen. "Gave it to me when we landed but...ah there we are!" He grinned at Rydian. "They should be along momentarily to help with your..." the man faltered as he looked at Serena and Aiden and finally seemed to realise who—or what—they were, "guests..." He finished lamely.

"Captain...sorry, I don't think I ever asked your name?"

"Briggs, sir."

"Captain Briggs, this is Serena and Aiden Levaanton. Aiden used to rule this city, before the conquest. And Serena almost killed me the first time we met. Serena, Aiden, this is the captain of the ship that brought me back to Talamh."

"Ah, nice to meet your acquaintance?" Serena said faintly.

She wasn't sure if it was appropriate, given the circumstances, but she offered her hand. The man's eyes had practically doubled in size at their introduction, but his manners kicked in and he clasped her fingers in a quick shake. Briggs looked at her father next, but when Aiden made no move to extend any greetings, the man turned back to Rydian.

"It...it wasn't a joke earlier, was it?" His voice came out more like a whisper. Seemed like he was losing his voice. "On the ship, when you said they built these towers?"

"No." Rydian gave a wry smile. He cast a glance around the corridor. "In fact, if I'm not mistaken, I believe this was actually *their* tower, before the Federation claimed it."

If the man's eyes had been large before, they practically bulged from his face now. "How...how is that possible?"

Before Rydian could reply, the sound of running footsteps approached from around the nearby corner. Rydian immediately went tense, but it was only the servants the captain had requested. Three women and two men slowed to a brisk walk when they turned the bend and found the four of them waiting. They wore plain white clothes and bowed their heads in a human gesture of respect as they approached.

"Ah...someone called for us?" one of the men announced, before adding a belated, "sirs."

Serena's stomach twisted at the sight of yet more humans in her family's tower. She eyed the newcomers as Rydian spoke, trying to keep the feelings from her face. Not that humans were particularly good at reading Alfurian emotions.

"Yes," Rydian said, gesturing to Serena and her father. "I'd like you to find quarters for my guests and ensure they are bathed and clothed. I'll..." He paused as the captain gave a suggestive cough. "Yes, Briggs?"

"Oh, I just thought I should mention, sir, that there are a few documents you'll need to complete before you settle in."

Rydian rolled his eyes. "Spare me the Federation's bureaucracy." He sighed. "Sure. We can go over security arrangements while we're at it."

Turning, he placed a hand on Serena's shoulder. She shivered at his touch. She could *feel* the Light prickling her, even through skin and cloth. Even when he wasn't actively using it. He felt like a furnace.

"These people will take care of you," he said, offering a reassuring smile. "My arrival was a bit unorthodox, so I guess there's a few things I still need to take care of. I'll come and find you in a bit." He looked again at the servants. "Take care of my friends here. Give them what-ever they need."

With that, he moved away with the captain, leaving Serena and her father alone with the servants. The second the pair vanished, the humans lost their subservient manner. Their manners altogether, for that matter.

"Aarf, they stink!"

"Disgusting things."

"What the hell does he want them for?"

"Oh, I know what he wants *this* one for," another chuckled. She caught Serena by the arm and squeezed.

Serena tried to pull away, but it seemed even these

lowly servants had enough imbued Light to resist her strength.

"Ooh, this one thinks she's a fighter," the woman mocked. "Come on you little brat, let's get you cleaned up or your master will never want to touch you." She laughed again.

"What should we do with the old one, Val?" One of the men poked a finger at her father's chest. Aiden shrank away, retreating back into himself.

A growl rumbled from Serena's chest. "You leave my father alone!"

The humans turned towards her, eyes wide with surprise.

Thwack.

Serena stumbled as the woman they'd called Val struck her across the face. It hadn't been a particularly hard blow. But she hadn't seen it coming, and in her still weakened state, it was enough to stagger her.

"Geeze, the Alfur in these parts are mouthy, aren't they? No wonder they don't let us on the surface. Marcus, you and Bud take that old one off and get him tidied up. The boss obviously brought him to keep his mistress happy. Missy and I will deal with mouthy here. What, oh toughen up you little brat, I barely touched you."

A growl had rumbled from Serena's throat at the blow. She bit it back and straightened, eyes shooting daggers at the woman who'd struck her. It was nothing compared to the blows she'd received in the arena—or even from the guards in their cells. She wasn't about to show weakness now. Though...

...it did hurt. Not physically so much, but the crack to her spirit. For the briefest of moments, she'd actually allowed herself to believe they had found sanctuary, that Rydian had pulled them from the flames.

Of course he had other motivations.

She struggled to keep the shame from her face as the men led her father away. If this was what it took to keep him safe from that man in the arena...

A lump lodged in her throat. She hadn't even had a chance to ask her father about the man, what he had wanted, how he had known them. She watched as he disappeared around a corner in the corridor, head bowed, defeated. The last six months had broken him. Nothing remained of the prince he'd once been.

Then again, nothing remained now of the woman *she* had been before the conquest.

Imprisonment had left them both a hollow shell of their former selves.

She said nothing as the woman grasped her arm so hard it hurt and practically dragged her in the opposite direction of her father. Head bowed, she allowed her mind to drift. It was an escape she'd often used in their cell, to distract herself from the nightmare she'd found herself within. This time though...

...doors hissed and she gasped as heavy hands pushed her from behind, propelling her into the chamber.

"Out of those clothes," Val snapped, the embodiment

of impatience. "I'll not have that stink fouling up the place another second longer."

Serena staggered a few steps before recovering her balance. Only then did she realise where she was. This was *her* chambers, her own rooms, from before the conquest. Her hearts twisted into the depths of her abdomen.

Of all the places they could have brought her, why did it have to be *here?* The place where she'd grown to adulthood, where she'd spent so many days in quiet contemplation—and outright raging against her father. This had been where she'd plotted with the other Alfurian heirs against the council of Princes, schemed to raise up the humans, to free them...

She closed her eyes. Those memories were dust in the Talamh wind now. She'd been a child then, a teenager raging against the unfairness of the world. Now...now she would do anything to return to those innocent days.

To her horror, she felt a hot tear streak her cheek.

"Oh for the Light's sake, the brat is crying."

This time Serena sensed the blow coming. It made little difference. She'd used most of what Rydian had given her to accelerate her healing—and this time Val put her own Light behind her hand. Red flashed across Serena's vision as the woman's palm struck her hard across the face.

"Into the bathing chamber," the growl followed. "Don't make me ask a third time."

Serena forced herself to bite back the harsh words on her tongue. They would only earn her further retribution.

Besides, the thought of entering her shower pod and washing the filth of months from her skin had her hearts racing. The closest she'd come to bathing since the conquest was the day a hose had been brought into the prison to spray them down with cold water. She'd felt half-drowned by the end—and not a great deal cleaner.

So doing her best not to think about *why* she was bathing, Serena stripped off her clothes—which were basically rotting rags by now—and stepped into the bathing chamber. Without her Manus reader, she didn't have control over the apparatus, but another hiss came from behind as Val activated it for her.

Boiling hot jets of water burst from the sides and ceiling. Yelping, the women retreated back into the bedchamber, leaving her alone in the steam. Serena sighed, dropping her head and closing her eyes, surrendering to the warmth. The heat would have been enough to sear a human's skin, but to her it was only a pleasant needling sensation. The soaps and oils mixed into the water helped to soften the grime caked onto her. Even then, it took long minutes of scrubbing before her skin regained its transparent shine.

A shame the scars left by her battles could not be so easily removed. Each fight in the arena had left their mark, for she hadn't had the Light to spare to heal her wounds afterwards. They'd had to heal the traditional way, so that every cut and scrap would remain forever as reminder of the battles she'd fought—and won.

Finally she was clean, but she still couldn't leave the

heat, the warmth. Standing under the jets, she could almost pretend, almost convince herself it had all been a dream, that the terrible months had been just a nightmare, that she would step from the falling water and things would be like before. Her father directing the council, she and her friends arguing for more protections for the humans...

Serena bit back a sob as the flow of water spluttered and died. It needed more Light, but without her Manus reader, she couldn't direct it correctly into the panel. Steeling herself, she turned and stepped back into the main chamber.

She was surprised to find herself alone. Her grumpy caretakers had vanished—along with her clothes. Not that they really deserved the title at this point. She found in their place a scarlet shift of fine silk draped over the bedcovers. Her cheeks paled when she picked it up and saw it was so fine as to leave very little to the imagination.

Before the conquest, the Alfur on Talamh had little embarrassment in nudity—and certainly not around humans. But that had been before, when *they* had been the ones in the position of power. In control of their own fate. Now...this shift seemed to scream a message, to serve as a reminder she was no longer in control of her own fate.

She drew in a breath and thought about her father. Defeated he might be, but Rydian had given him Light and freed him from the cage. The human had saved him—saved them both. If this was the cost...

Exhaling, Serena slipped into the shift. Her skin was

raw from the scrubbing and tingled at the soft touch of the fabric. With nothing else to do, she started towards the bed, before thinking better of it. She was so exhausted, the second her head touched the pillow she would be out. She...she wanted to be awake, when Rydian came. At least then...at least she could guarantee her father's safety, before...

Feeling the blood draining from her face, Serena chose the sofa. If she'd had a mirror, Serena imagined she must look a ghost. She shouldn't be embarrassed, she knew. She understood the mechanics of what was expected of her, that their...biologies were similar enough to perform... those acts. Though no Alfur she knew of had ever considered the idea. And having evolved from entirely different developmental pathways and planets, procreation would be impossible. That much she was grateful for...

Serena jumped as the door hissed open. The Light in the room was dimmed and Rydian paused in the doorway, blinking as he struggled to adjust from the brilliance outside. Serena was grateful for the second to compose herself. She'd thought herself ready, but the sight of Rydian standing there, the one human she had ever trusted...

She found herself strangely flustered.

Rubbing his eyes, Rydian finally stepped into the room and made a gesture at the door. Light burst from his palm and it slid closed with a hiss. These humans really didn't know how to operate Alfurian technology. The towers were designed to be efficient and soundless, not use a metric tonne of Light. Still, Serena had larger concerns just now, like ensuring her father's protection.

Drawing in a breath, she rose from the sofa. "Rydian, before—"

"Arg!"

Rydian leapt practically a foot in the air and exploded with Light. The brilliance emanating from his skin obliterated every shadow in the room. For a second, Serena thought he would strike her, he looked so shocked to find her standing there. Blinking, he finally seemed to register who it was in the room with him.

Serena dropped her head, unable to meet the man's glowing eyes. In doing so, she got another glimpse of her shift. She could have died of embarrassment. His Light had turned it completely transparent now, robbing her of whatever shred of modesty she'd left.

"Serena?" he said at last, sounding somewhat breathless. "I...what...I didn't expect..."

Serena scrunched her eyes closed. Enough of this. "It's okay," she said, her voice hoarse. Gathering her courage, she forced herself to meet his eyes. "I understand. I'm willing." She took a step towards him. Only a foot separated them now. She reached out a tentative hand for his. "I just...just need you to promise my father...will be taken care of..." Her voice broke, and her courage wilted. Her eyes fell back to the ground. The carpet was soft beneath her bare feet. She had enjoyed that sensation, once. Now... now she barely noticed it.

A shiver ran across her spine. To her horror, she felt

the tears building in her eyes again. She blinked, and a hot tear slid across her cheek. *No, no, no!* She couldn't mess this up. She had to...had to go through with it. Trembling, she reached for the tie of her shift, fingers fumbling for the knot. He wouldn't...wouldn't notice tears, if she...

Strong hands caught hers. "Serena, stop." There was concern in Rydian's voice. "What are you doing?"

"Please, just let me...I can be...what you want." Her head jerked up. She met his eyes through the tears. His face blurred as she struggled to keep them from falling. She saw the frown twist his lips, the crease to his forehead. He wasn't happy. She tried for the ties again, but he still held her.

"No," he ordered. "Stop. Wait here."

Then he turned and left, leaving Serena once more alone in the room.

Despair overwhelmed her as she realised she'd failed. This had been her one chance to save herself and her father. Pulling her knees up to her chest, Serena Levaanton buried her head in her arms and wept.

EIGHT

RYDIAN FOUND CAPTAIN HIGGS STILL SITTING IN THE meeting room where he'd left the man half an hour before. Stalking across the room, he struggled to control the shaking in his hands—and the broiling Light beneath his skin. Not since he'd suffered the unending screams of the Haze had Rydian felt so angry.

Surprise showed on the captain's face when he looked up from his paperwork and found Rydian standing there.

"Private Holt, I thought—"

"The servants," Rydian spoke before he exploded. "Where are they?"

"The servants, sir?"

"The ones who went with Serena. I want to speak with them."

"Ah...I would guess they're already sleeping, sir. It's quite la—"

"Wake them."

Without another word, Rydian took a seat at the table. If he hadn't, he might have drove his hand through the steel-panelled walls. He didn't offer any further explanation, trusting the scowl on his face to convey his mood. Higgs seemed to get the message. Leaping to his feet, he fumbled in his pockets for the control tablet and began mashing buttons.

Rydian sighed. He should have asked for one of those earlier—then he wouldn't have needed to drag Briggs into the coming conflict. He'd already created more work for the man than he'd needed to by teleporting from the bridge of the ship. And he seemed like a decent sort. Better than the damned servants staffing this place, that was for certain.

Leaning back in his chair, he ran his hands through his hair and found they were still trembling. He clenched them into fists—one of Light, one of flesh. Damn the Federation and their indoctrination. The servants here were from off-world. Of *course* they would interpret his instructions like this. After all, what other reason could a member of the Federation Armed Forces have for bringing an *Alfur* into his accommodations. Not like they could possibly be a friend or advisor or anything *meaningful.*

A lump rose in his throat. The image of Serena, lit by the glow of his Light, lingered...of her pressing up against him, only the thin silken shift between them. Blood pounded against his temples as he remembered the stirring in his chest...

...and again he felt the guilt when he saw the first tear fall, when he noticed the fear in her golden eyes.

Godsdamnit!

He stood abruptly and began to pace. The captain shot a worried glance in his direction, then returned his eyes to the tablet. Hopefully something was happening.

Forcing himself to take a calming breath, Rydian crossed to the window. The sight of Goma, his home, offered him some calm. This was what he was fighting for. Not for the world they'd had before. And certainly not for the Federation.

A smile touched his face as a memory came to him, one from his months at the academy. There had been an old hound at the training facility, not much different to Aureli's mutt. She'd had a litter while he was there. The memory of the blind and helpless puppies tumbling over one another while the cadets at the facility laughed was strangely calming. Just the idea of keeping such creatures as pets in Goma would have been considered insanity when the Haze still stretched over the planet.

Elsewhere, animals, pets, they were as normal as breathing.

Talamh could have that, now the Haze was gone. That, and so much more.

That was what he wanted. A Talamh better than the one the Alfur had created, and the one the Federation wanted.

"Sir?"

Rydian started. Looking up, he saw that the captain

had been joined by a trio of sleepy looking women in their nightclothes.

"These are the women you asked for, sir."

Allowing his anger to show, Rydian strode across the room to stand before them. He wasn't surprised to see the fear in their eyes. Why not? They'd just been dragged from their beds in the middle of the night, to be confronted by a member of the Federation Armed Forces. He clenched his fists. This was not where he should be concentrating his attention just now. But he couldn't let this mistake happen again.

"It seems you have misunderstood my orders."

"Sir?" The larger of the two women spoke. "We placed the courtesan in your chambers, as you requested. If she is not to your liking, I would only be too happy to find another—"

"Her name is Serena," Rydian interrupted, "and she is *not* here as my courtesan. I told you to treat her with respect..." he sighed, noticing the confusion in the women's eyes. They couldn't understand. Or wouldn't. "Just...what was done with Serena's father? Has he been fed and clothed?"

"It's an Alfur, sir," the woman replied, "they don't need no food."

"*He* is called Aiden Levaanton," Rydian snapped, "and you will provide him with Light and a chamber in which to sleep. You will also convey your deepest regrets for any mistreatment he has experienced in this tower. I will visit him in the morning, and if he has a single word of complaint, I will see you all evacuated from this tower from the highest floor. Now *go!*"

"Yes, sir!" Terrified, the women fled.

Silence followed as the doors closed with a whisper behind them. Only the captain remained. With a sigh, Rydian turned to the man.

"You have questions?"

"Things really are different here, aren't they?" Briggs said. He wore a contemplative look on his face. "That Alfur, Aiden Levaa...ton, will you really let me speak with him in the morning?"

Despite the late hour and his earlier encounter, Rydian found himself smiling at the man's enthusiasm.

"Of course, captain. I appreciate everything you've done here." He paused. "For now...it ah, seems my bedchamber has already been assigned to another. Does your tablet show any others available?" He hadn't missed that the room he'd found Serena in was her old one. And he wasn't about to kick her out in the middle of the night, after what had happened.

"All of the bedchambers on this floor have been cleaned and prepped for visitors, sir, so theoretically any of them should be available for your use."

"Thank you, captain. I'll leave you to your work then."

He wandered back through the empty corridors, mind drifting back six months, to when he and Hazel had snuck into this very tower to find Serena. Their plan had been simple—free the Alfur from her father's containment and have her lead them to her people's secret weakness. With that in hand, they would finally be able to negotiate an equal peace between their peoples.

Instead, well, the humans of Talamh had gotten everything they'd ever wanted, in a twisted kind of sense.

Without realising it, Rydian found himself once more outside Serena's door. He hesitated. There were other doors here. He could retreat to one of them and finally have some rest, rather than face the Alfurian princess. But...no, he needed to check on her, to explain it had all been a misunderstanding...

...though his mind couldn't help but return to that image, to those golden eyes, her soft, translucent skin...

Shaking himself, Rydian drew in a breath and flooded the control panel with Light. The doors hissed loudly as he entered.

A pale face looked up from the floor, illuminated by the glow from the corridor. His heart panged when he saw the tears in Serena's eyes. Biting his lip, he allowed the doors to close, the gloom covering the thinness of Serena's shift. Another mistake he needed to correct. Damn, he should have thought to send for proper clothes earlier.

Crossing to the bed, Rydian pulled off the covers and moved to crouch beside the young Alfur, drawing the blankets around her. She hadn't cared about nudity, the last time he'd mistakenly encountered her in somewhat-less-than-clothed state, but things had obviously changed.

"I checked on your father," he said, drawing her to her feet with the blanket wrapped around her. "They'll treat you both properly from now on. We can meet with him in the morning."

"I...thank you," she whispered, bowing her head. "I'm sorry...if I caused offence—"

"You did nothing wrong," Rydian said quicky. "The women...misunderstood my intentions. I should have known it would happen. Those of the Federation...they are used to such...things."

Serena was watching him through narrowed eyes, as though she couldn't quite bring herself to believe him. At least she kept the blanket wrapped around her this time. It made it much easier for Rydian to concentrate.

"You are sure?" she said at last, still hesitant. "My father, he's all I have left...I'm willing if...if that's what..."

Rydian's heart panged at the pain in her voice. Gods, this wasn't the Serena he'd met sword to sword in the arena all those months ago. He wished he could have returned sooner, prevented this. He wanted to say that, and so much more, but...it didn't change the truth. He'd failed her. Her, and so many others who had suffered while he'd been gone.

"I only want to help you, Serena."

"Why?" The question was so soft, he almost missed it. She seemed to realise it and looked away, before she continued. "Why are you helping us? You know what my people did to yours. What *I* would have done to you, that night..." She swallowed, seeming to struggle for words. "I wish I could say that I would not have done it..." She looked at him, and now he saw the pain in her golden eyes.

"But I can't. I would have killed you, Rydian. I would have cut you down to save us all."

Well, that was...frank.

His mind snapped back to that night, to Serena standing over him, sword in hand. It would be a lie to say he hadn't thought about that moment. Trapped in the Haze, tormented by his own Light and driven to the point of insanity...he'd been helpless.

Steeling himself, Rydian forced those memories from his mind—and a smile to his lips.

"I know," he murmured, "and I don't blame you, after everything I've seen since." He looked at her. "I'm sorry for what's happened here. If they hadn't taken me..." He signed. "No, much as I might wish it, I couldn't have stopped this. I wasn't strong enough. I'm *still* not strong enough." He met Serena's gaze. "The Federation...the forces they have at their command...they're invincible, Serena."

"It's okay," she whispered, though her eyes told him it wasn't. How could it be? "It's the way...of things."

It might be the way of things now, but it hadn't been before, at least not for Talamh. Here, they had found a way to suppress the Light humanity had used to conquer the galaxy. Not just that, but to harvest it, to turn it to the benefit of the planet, and create technologies that far surpassed anything he'd witnessed amongst the Federation.

But none of that mattered now, and all Rydian could offer Serena was a nod.

Still…

"It doesn't have to be."

Her lips tightened, but the Alfurian princess said nothing. He could see it in her eyes, the defeat that weighed upon her shoulders. It was a look Rydian was all too familiar with, after his time in the arena. The look of someone who knows they're only one battle away from the cold embrace of the grave.

"It's true," he insisted. "I…" he trailed off.

I have a plan.

That was what he wanted to say, but Rydian knew better than to speak the words aloud. There was at least one powerful Lightmaker on the planet. Nothing could be discounted, however impossible it might seem. Even eaves-dropping here, in this quiet place above the world…

He blinked, realising he'd allowed his mind to drift. But when he opened his mouth to say more, he found the Alfurian princess's eyes closed, her head cradled gently against her hands. A soft snort came from her lips. Rydian found himself smiling. Exhaustion weighed heavily on him, but he sat there on the floor a while, glad one of them at least had found some peace.

Eventually, he lifted Serena gently in his arms and carried her to the bed. She mumbled something at his touch, but did not wake. Her scent drifted in his nostrils, a kind of rosy fragrance. It made his heart beat faster. Lowering her onto the sheets, he paused, watching the gentle rise and fall of her chest. She must have really been exhausted, to drift off so completely. How long since she'd had a full night's sleep?

He lingered another second, then turned and slipped out the door. Despite his words with the captain, Rydian sensed his time was less than he'd hoped. He couldn't afford to rest, at least not yet.

It was time for him to visit some old friends.

NINE

Reclining in the busted up chair in the corner of the shack he shared with Jasmine Holt, Johanas stroked the enormous head of the giant cat, Fatimah. Rydian had bonded with the creature when he'd been exiled to the jungles of the continent, but that had been broken when the Federation had taken Rydian off-world. Johanas had adopted the beast in the chaotic days afterwards, and while they'd never formed the same depth of connection, he still occasionally sensed ripples of the big cat's emotions.

And what Fatimah felt just now was apprehension.

Even without the bond, that much was obvious. Her fur stood on end, making the already enormous beast practically loom in the little room, and every so often she would let out a little growl. Once that sound might have been enough to send Johanas scurrying for cover, but now he continued to pet the great cat, offering what comfort he could.

Truth be told, he felt that same sense of apprehension, that sinking dread one experienced when standing at the edge of a cliff. After months of calm, the winds of change were blowing once more on Talamh.

And they had arrived in the form of Rydian Holt.

Johanas glanced in the direction of the tiny kitchen where Jasmine was cooking a late supper. Her lost son's sudden reappearance was all anyone was talking about in Goma. A lot of people were angry, of course. Rydian had stolen Serena and Aiden Levaanton right out from under the queen's nose, after all. Hazel couldn't be happy about that development. His stomach twisted at the thought of his friend, alone in one of those towers, but she had chosen her path, and it was one he could not follow her down.

No, his greater concern was Jasmine. He'd expected her to be overjoyed at Rydian's sudden return from the grave, but she hadn't said a word about it.

Another rumble came from Fatimah. Johanas made a cooing sound, but this time there was no calming the beast. Suddenly she was on her feet, eyes burning with the glow of Light, fixed on a point on the floor several feet from where he sat—

Whoosh.

Johanas cried out as a fiery burst of Light condensed in the centre of the room, before it flickered out as quickly as it had appeared, leaving in its place...

"Rydian!"

He was out of his chair and halfway across the room before his friend had a chance to see him coming. Crashing into Rydian, he wrapped the man in a hug that would have crushed lesser men. As it was, Rydian barely managed to cry out for mercy between bursts of laughter. Then he was hugging Johanas back, his embrace only slightly less crushing, despite Rydian's much smaller size.

Both wore grins from ear to ear as they stepped back and looked one another up and down.

"The Light looks good on you," Johanas remarked.

It was true. Rydian had always been small, and while his skill and dedication made up for the lack of muscle in the arena, now his body could have been chiselled from marble. No more did he look to be on the edge of malnutrition. Lithe muscles and the hard edge to his jaw spoke of a power and confidence he'd lacked before.

Rydian chuckled. "I see peace has been good for you as well."

Johanas clapped a hand on Rydian's shoulders. Without any reason to train anymore, he had indeed put on a few pounds. "Still strong enough to tear you in two if you don't watch that mouth, my friend," he said good naturedly.

A rumble from Fatimah drew Rydian's attention to the big cat. He crouched as the creature approached, reaching out a hand to stroke the enormous head. No words passed between them—at least not out loud—but after a moment Rydian rose once more and nodded to Johanas.

"She says you have cared for her and my mother. Thank you for that, my friend."

"Least I could do."

"Ahem."

The pair turned as a cough came from behind them. Jasmine stood in the doorway to the kitchen, arms crossed, face impassive.

The smile fell from Rydian's lips. "Mum," he whispered.

Johanas swallowed. He understood the yearning in Rydian's voice. Jasmine Holt was supposed to be dead, killed in a botched resistance action a year before the conquest. But when Hazel and Rydian had gone to the Alfurian tower in search of the Alfur's weakness, they'd found Jasmine instead. She had been the first to discover the truth—that beyond Talamh, it was humanity who ruled the galaxy, not the Alfur. She had betrayed her fellow resistance members to hide that truth and gone over to the Alfur.

"Son." Jasmine's voice was strangely harsh, cold. "Where have you been?"

Rydian lifted his chin. "Learning."

"Ay. I imagine the Federation had a lot to teach you." The woman clenched her fist, and Rydian's eyes flickered to the Manus reader she still wore.

"They did." He cast his eyes around the room, then frowned, as only just now realising where he was. He moved to the window and looked out onto the quiet street.

"It's strange, being in this house without dad. Why did you come here?"

Johanas swallowed at the mention of the man. He had died on the sands of the arena, when Rydian and Hazel had intervened in Johanas's fight. A fight he would have lost, had *intended* to lose, if not for his friends.

"Was there somewhere else you expected me to go?" Jasmine asked.

"Didn't Hazel—"

"She offered. I declined."

"*We* declined," Johanas added.

Rydian's frown deepened. "I don't understand," he said, eyes fixed on Jasmine. "You...hate her, don't you? Why? If not for her...she helped you...helped to save me."

Jasmine looked away. "A moment of weakness that I will regret for the rest of my life."

Johanas saw the flicker pain that crossed Rydian's face.

"I should have...should have let them do it," she continued, eyes fixed pointedly on the brick walls. "Better to see you dead than this. Than watching my son become a pawn of the Federation. To see you become a soldier in their armies.

The colour drained slowly from Rydian's face. Even Johanas was surprised at the venom in Jasmine's words— and he had seen her bitterness for himself these last six months. He felt for his friend, to hear such loathing in the voice of his mother. Still, Rydian said nothing, only stood at the window and watched his mother, waiting.

Finally her head swung around, and their eyes met.

"Why did they send you here, Rydian?" she demanded. "To root out any resistance? To spy on your own people, your own family, on their behalf? Why? There has to be a reason."

"No one sent me, mum," Rydian whispered, and Johanas could see the way his eyes shimmered, the pain he held back. Letting out a sigh, he turned from the window. "Funny, how many people think the world would have been a better place if I'd died that day. Still, I didn't think you'd be one of them, mum."

Jasmine said nothing, but now Johanas noticed how she failed to meet her son's eyes.

"Never mind. It hardly matters now. That's not why I came."

"Why are you here, Rydian?" Johanas asked.

"To share what I've learned from the Federation."

"We have no interest in their murderous ways," Jasmine spat.

"Of course not," Rydian finally seemed to snap. "You gave up on your own people a long time ago, didn't you? I shouldn't have expected anything more of you."

Johanas stood awkwardly by as the two faced off. A soft head nudged his hand as the leopard came to his side. He could sense her discomfort. *You and me both, Fatimah.*

"I didn't give up. I saw the truth, the monsters we truly were—"

"You saw a glimpse of what *the Federation* have made of the galaxy. But you haven't seen it all. You haven't seen the people out there on other planets, living normal lives, doing their best to make ends meet. They're not so different to us."

"That's the problem. We're all monsters, Rydian. All of us, and them. Humanity. Can you really look at what's become of your friend, the hatred that consumes her, and claim otherwise?" Jasmine paused, her chest heaving, eyes wide. Slowly her shoulders fell as the fight went out of her. "Why are we even discussing this?" she whispered. "It's over. The monsters won. Go back to whatever you've been doing, Rydian. To fighting for your beloved humans. You're no son of mine."

Johanas's blood ran cold at her words. There was no venom in them now, only a sick despair.

Not that it mattered to Rydian. His eyes were hard as he looked at her.

"Gods, do you really think so little of me?"

Turning, he staggered across to the sofa and sank into cushions. The overextended springs squealed at the movement.

Letting out a long breath, Johanas looked from his friend to Jasmine. When she said nothing, he wandered over to Rydian and stood before the man. Fatimah followed and nudged her head against Rydian's knee. Some of the tension drained from him as he scratched the big cat's ears. The soft rumble of her purrs filled the room.

"You're not here with the Federation, are you?" Johanas said softly. Jasmine didn't know her son like he did.

"No."

"Do you plan to join the resistance?"

"Resistance?" Rydian exhaled softly. "What resistance?"

"Johanas..." There was a warning in Jasmine's tone.

Johanas ignored her. "There are some in the city who whisper the Federation are no better than the Alfurian princes. I've even heard whispers of Alfur who escaped during the conquest, ones lying low in the cities or who escaped into the wilds. If we could gather them, maybe we could stop Hazel—"

"No."

"Rydian, I know she was our friend..."

"It's not that..."

Johanas frowned when his friend didn't continue. Rydian's head was bowed, his hand still on the big cat's head. He seemed...tired.

"Then what, Rydian?" Johanas asked. He didn't want to fight, to be responsible for yet more death, but... "Maybe there are good people out there, Rydian, but that's just it. They're somewhere out there." He gestured at the ceiling. "They can't help us. And Rydian, however much Hazel might be trying, the truth is things are as bad as they've ever been in Goma."

"Tell me."

"Its...it's the Light. Now everyone has it. But no one is trained. No one is in control. Disagreements, fights, even crime, it's all taken on a deadlier edge than it ever had with the Alfur. I think Hazel is trying to organise a security force to patrol the city, but it's a dangerous job and few are eager to stick up their hands."

Rydian exhaled. "I understand. But...it can't be like it was before. Rulers and resistance. Uprisings and revolution. One side falling, only for the other to rise and repeat the cycle of abuse."

"Humanity deserves to fall," Jasmine cut in.

Johanas ground his teeth but said nothing.

"Probably," Rydian whispered, "but the Federation won't be defeated. Not by us. Not even if all of Talamh rose against them, we couldn't hold a candle to their power."

"Just like I thought—"

"*Enough!*" Rydian exploded. Rising from the sofa, he crossed to stand before his mother. "*I'm* talking now. You've had your chance. You failed. Worse, you turned against your own people. Your own *son*." His voice cracked. "It's my turn. I'm going to show us all a better way."

"How?" Johanas asked.

"Here." Rydian tossed Johanas a tablet of glass and steel. "You can use that to order a transport to the Levaanton tower. I'm calling a meeting. Tomorrow at noon. I'll explain once everyone is there."

He turned to go, but a rumble from Fatimah drew him back. He held out a hand, and the cat stalked over and rubbed its enormous head against his fingers.

Both vanished in a flash of brilliant Light.

TEN

Rydian did not return directly to his tower after the visit with Johanas and his mother. The confrontation had left him feeling empty and hollow. His mother's corrosive words lingered in his mind, undermining his confidence. If she could believe such things about him, could think him so weak...did he really have what it took to take on the Federation?

A pulse of reassurance carried across his bond with Fatimah. He sensed a flickering of images, scenes of his mother standing at the window, staring at the stars. Through the images came a sense of yearning, of sorrow. He swallowed, resting a hand on the big cat's head.

Thank you for caring for them while I was gone.

Yet the big cat's reassurance was not enough, and he found the images only made the hurt sting all the more for what he'd lost.

He brought them to the rooftop of the arena. It was the

tallest building in the lower city, and while still only an ant hill beside the glory of the Alfurian towers, he savoured the view. Many an afternoon he had sat on other rooftops, looking out over the familiar glow of the city—though now the fiery glow of lanterns had been replaced with the steady luminescence of Light.

The sight reminded him of Johanas's words. Had Light really made the lives of those in this city worse, as his friend said? He could still remember the struggle of his own family to heat their home in the winter on the meagre rations of coal provided by the Alfur. Surely at least some of that misery had been lifted.

He sighed, his mood low. That...that hadn't been the reunion he'd been expecting. For so long, he'd thought his mother dead. Then at the moment they'd been reunited, the Haze had almost destroyed him, and the Federation had stolen him away. Now, this night, had finally been their chance. *His* chance. To feel her arms around him again. To hold her tight, feel the warmth of her love.

Instead, he'd been met with cold, uncaring hatred.

His heart ached with the weight of loss. Not just for his mother's betrayal, but for his father too. It had been strange to find his mother and Johanas living in their house, the last refuge he'd had with his father, before Rydian had messed everything up. So much had changed since then. Those days seemed so simple now, his father's advice so wise. If only he had listened, and just kept his head down instead of raging against Alfurian authority, so much might have been different.

But none of that mattered now. His father was dead, his mother a shadow of her former self. For better or worse, this world needed Rydian to take charge. Somehow, the fate of the planet was his to decide, his roll of the dice to throw.

It would be a terrible gamble. He had little to lose at this point, but these people, those living their lives beneath the shadow of the soaring towers, it was their lives he would risk. If he failed, the Federation might decide this planet wasn't worth the risk and annihilate everyone. Yet if he succeeded...

That was the thing, wasn't it? He could do nothing, and nothing would change. The people of Goma would continue with their lives, toiling day in and day out for enough to feed and clothe themselves, persevering while those above grew rich off the fruits of their labours.

Didn't they deserve better than that? Didn't they deserve a chance to dream, to transpire to something greater in their lives? A chance for freedom, to rise from the dirt and build a better world for themselves and their children?

Exhaling, Rydian sat up. At his side, Fatimah stirred, sensing the same ripple in the world as he had. Nearby, reality shifted, followed by a burst of Light. Rydian's mouth was dry as he watched the man step from nowhere to land on the roof. A rumble came from Fatimah, but Rydian raised a hand and bid the beast calm through their connection.

It was the man from the arena, the one determined to

kill Serena and Aiden. Rydian hadn't expected to find him up and walking so soon after his blow, let alone Light-jumping. A shiver ran down Rydian's spine as he peered at the man's core and sensed the power there. This was a dangerous man.

But the Federation general made no move to attack. Clasping his hands behind his back, he wandered over to join them at the edge of the rooftop.

"General," Rydian greeted.

"Rydian Holt, I take it?" the man murmured. He didn't look in Rydian's direction, but gazed out over the shimmering lights of the city.

He inclined his head. "I wasn't expecting a visit from you until tomorrow."

"Tomorrow is almost upon us."

"I suppose it is." Rydian couldn't keep the tension from his voice now.

The general seemed to sense it, for turning, he finally looked Rydian in the eye. "Will it be war then?"

Rydian clenched his fists, allowing a trickle of Light to gather there, though he was by no means certain this was a fight he could win. He'd taken the man by surprise earlier, put everything into the blow, yet the general didn't have a scratch on him.

A smile cracked the man's harsh expression and he chuckled. "Relax, lad, I did not come here for a fight."

Still Rydian did not back down. "With respect then, general, why have you come?"

"Please, call me Colley. We both know I'm here off the

books. And I thought my reasons for coming here were rather self-explanatory."

Rydian grimaced. "Let me clarify—what are you doing on my planet?"

"Your planet?"

"Talamh is the only home I've ever known."

"You will know many more, lad," Colley replied. "I heard of your progress at the academy before I came here, and wondered. Now I know for sure. You have been blessed with a gift. Only once in a generation do I see a Lightmaker rise with such potency."

"Perhaps I was only determined to pass your tests so I could return home. I...wasn't sure what I would find here."

"Ay, your queen filled me in on some of your planet's history." His gaze shifted to the towers that loomed above them. "Hard to believe a bunch of Alfur found the mettle for conquest. Haven't seen that in several generations. You must hold a great deal of hate in your heart for their kind. Is that why you took my prey—to have your own measure of revenge?"

"Perhaps."

"Are you always a man of such few words, lad?"

Rydian said nothing, before a grin split his lips. "I suppose I am."

Had Johanas or Hazel been there at that moment, they would have laughed their heads off.

"No matter," Colley rumbled. "You speak of this planet as your home, but you do not yet understand just what you are. How many years of life have you enjoyed on this backwater planet? Twenty?" He crossed his arms. "Ah, I hardly remember such innocent days now, so much time has passed. What would you guess at my age, lad?"

Rydian looked at the man. His short-cropped hair and beard were streaked with grey and the skin at the corners of his lips wrinkled when he spoke, but he would not think the general older than his father. He shrugged.

"Fifty?"

The general chuckled. "Just a few months ago I marked my eight hundredth year."

"*What?*"

"That is a secret we do not advertise so openly, lad," Colley said, placing a heavy hand on Rydian's shoulder. "Even amongst humanity, there are differences in our innate Light. Some are particularly blessed. Those once in a generation talents like yourself or I, if given the opportunity to master their abilities, can escape even the cruel hand of time."

Rydian blinked. "But...Talamh...we're only..."

The general grimaced. "Yes. I was still a young man when your Alfur mutinied and stole our ships, and brought your ancestors to this planet."

"Then...you knew him, didn't you? Aiden Levaanton."

"Knew? Ha! Even then, one did not 'know' the Alfur. That is a corruption of this planet that must be expunged before we can bring your people into the fold of the Federation. They are animals, Rydian, consumed only by their hunger for Light. You of all people should know this. They had a chance at ruling this little planet, but instead they created a system designed to control you, to suppress your powers and harvest your Light. Meanwhile, a planet so rich in resources went wasted. You must have seen it from space—barely a fraction of its surface utilised. Such waste."

A growl came from Fatimah. The man cast the creature a glance and raised an eyebrow.

"Strange creatures this planet has bred. I have not seen so many Light-imbued animals in a single ecosystem before. No wonder the Alfur chose it for their little experiment."

"Aiden Levaanton claimed their efforts were a collaboration. Between their scientists and ours."

"And you believe that?"

Rydian paused. "He has lied before."

"Ay, they are a treacherous species. Tell me, if this planet, their Haze, truly was a work between our species, how was it your people ended enslaved, while theirs lived in their gilded towers?"

Pursing his lips, Rydian could only shake his head. Aiden had claimed the side-effects of the Haze hadn't been discovered until it was too late to correct, but the general was right. He only had the man's word on that. Still, he didn't say as much. He'd already said too much.

"You haven't answered my original question," he said instead. "What are Aiden and Serena Levaanton to you?"

Silence. Then the general sighed.

"The girl is no one, but yes, I 'knew' Aiden Levaanton. As much as one can know an Alfur. He was my daughter's lab assistant. One of the few we trusted with more than menial labour. A mistake we have since corrected, I might add."

"You hate him. Why?"

"Because he took my daughter from me."

Rydian stilled. "Took?"

"In his little mutiny. The ships that were taken, my daughter was amongst them."

"Ah," Rydian said, "now I see. You want vengeance."

A smile twisted Colley's lips. "And this surprises you?"

"No."

"Good," he paused. "I do not want conflict with a fellow Lightmaker. If you are willing to hand over the elder Aiden Levaanton, I will allow you to keep the daughter. I can even ensure the Federation does not question why one of their fresh recruits has such a creature in his employ. Much as I would savour Aiden's pain in watching his daughter perish, this is a sacrifice I am willing to pay, for the greater good."

"She will not be separated from him."

Colley's face darkened. "I will not be thwarted on this, lad. I am only offering you this chance because you show promise. The Federation needs those of your ilk. But this offer will not be made again."

Rydian drew in a breath. "I know, general."

"Then what is your decision?"

Above the distant rooftops, the first hints of light had appeared, the scarlet glow heralding in the new day. It shimmered on the great glass and steel structures that filled the sky, turning the city to blood.

"Give me until the end of the day," Rydian said at last. "So they can make their goodbyes. Then I will deliver the traitor to you myself."

The general watched him for a moment, as though he still expected some final request, but finally he nodded. "Very well."

He said nothing more, but turned and stepped off the rooftop, disappearing into the Light.

Rydian stood there a while longer, watching the eerie red glow of the sunrise. The colours still seemed off, without the Haze to taint the natural blue. Finally though, he sighed and gathered his power. He still had one more stop this evening before he returned to the tower. The one he dreaded most. But the effort had to be made.

Reaching out through the Light, he found the shimmer of Hazel's presence in another of the towers, and pulled himself through the abyss.

ELEVEN

Serena woke with a start, heart racing as the dreams clung to her. She'd been stumbling through the corridors of her home, trying to reach the control room for the Haze, to stop herself and the humans from reaching it. Time and time again, she would arrive in that hidden room, only to see herself looking back from the line of computers, a sad frown on her lips.

Then she would press a button, and the shimmer of the Haze would vanish...

...only for Serena to find herself again in the corridors, trying desperately to reach the control room, to stop...

Clenching her eyes closed, Serena placed a hand to her chest, trying to still the racing of her hearts. It hadn't happened like that, of course. It had been Hazel who had destroyed the console and broadcast the emergency message to bring the Federation, not her.

Though she might as well have. She'd led the woman there, after all.

Serena shivered. Lying there in the comfort of her own bed, she felt dirty, knowing that her people had suffered and died because of her. That her fellow Alfur were suffering even now, sleeping on cold stone floors, without blankets or cushions or even Light for sustenance. And here she was, enjoying the comforts of the enemy, sleeping in their beds, offering herself to them...

Throwing off the covers, she sat with her knees drawn up to her chest. But she couldn't stay like that, paralysed with fear and regret, unable to move forward, to escape the past. So sliding from the bed, she entered the bath chamber once more. At some point in the night she'd torn off the shift. Good riddance. Just looking at it made her feel dirty, like she was someone's plaything rather than an actual person. That had probably been the servant women's intent, she supposed, to show the Alfur her place.

She clenched her fists at the thought. Drawing her rage about herself, she drew the Light from her core and concentrated it in her fist. There was no Manus reader to direct its power, but holding her concentration, she placed her palm to the panel in the wall. It took all her concentration, but slowly the power filtered from her into the console, until *success!*

She closed her eyes as the boiling water engulfed her, enjoying the heat, the power of the jets. No human could suffer this heat, Light imbued or not, and she bathed in that knowledge for a moment. That despite everything, she was still stronger, still faster, than most of their kind. They would not break her.

Serena stayed like that for a half hour before the Light she'd fed the console ran out. The servants hadn't left her any towels, so she returned to the main chamber with the intention of using her bed sheets to dry herself. As she did, a *hiss* came from the entrance to her apartments. Someone was coming.

For a second, Serena felt an overwhelming need to scramble for the covers. To hide her nudity. Her shame.

But that was a *human* emotion. A *human* weakness.

She was Alfur.

And she was tired of kowtowing to the human condition.

So instead she lifted her chin and *glared* in the direction of the door.

Rydian entered, carrying a bundle in one hand and a glass of Light balanced in the other. He didn't notice her at first. She still had a chance to go for the covers. The pounding of her hearts screamed for her to do so.

Instead, Serena steeled herself. "You should really learn to knock, Rydian Holt."

She had to admit, there was a certain satisfaction in the way he stopped dead in his tracks. It wasn't every day you saw the powerful at a loss for words. Nor had she ever seen that shade of red on Rydian's cheeks.

"Sorry!" Rydian exclaimed, practically tripping over himself to turn around. "I thought you would still...didn't want to wake you...just wanted to leave some clothes...and Light!"

He staggered sideways and tripped over the sofa in a way that strongly suggested he had not only turned his back but also closed his eyes. Despite everything, Serena couldn't keep her mirth hidden. Her laughter rang from the walls as he stumbled again. But this time he almost spilled the Light, so padding forward on the balls of her feet, she reached around him and plucked the glass from his hands.

"Well in that case, thank you," she said, laughter in her voice.

The Light went down in a single gulp. Rydian was still mumbling something about being sorry. Smiling, she placed the glass back in his hand and took the bundle.

"Hope they're more to your liking." Rydian's voice followed her as she retreated to the bath chamber to change.

She smiled, warmed by the gesture of kindness—and his discomfort. It felt as though she'd recovered a little of something she'd lost the night before. Unwrapping the bundle, she found clothes similar to what she'd worn when she'd fought as the gladiator Rotin. Tight fitting, but with a firmness that suggested regular metal would struggle to cut through the dense fibres. It was perfect—except for the little Federation symbol on the front.

"It's a private's uniform," Rydian explained as she slipped into the tight-fitting pants and jacket. "I'm meant to wear it into battle, but I figure it suits you better than me."

Shrugging the jacket over her shoulders, Serena zipped up the front and gave herself a quick once over in the partially fogged up mirror. The metallic sheen was definitely some kind of protection against physical attacks, maybe even against weaker Light constructs. The joints were also stitched to give her plenty of movement.

"It's perfect," she said, returning to the main chamber. "Though I hope I won't be finding myself in battle anytime soon." She hesitated. "Unless there's something you're not telling me."

Ice trickled down her spine when she saw the grim look on Rydian's face. The embarrassment was gone now, and he was all business as he paced the room.

"I wish I could promise that, Serena," he said quietly, "but I didn't just return to Talamh to see old friends."

"Oh?" She arced an eyebrow, still watching his face. This...this was a different Rydian to the one she'd known, however briefly. He seemed older, more thoughtful.

Rydian shook his head. She said nothing as he wandered over to the sofa and took a seat.

"We can't beat them, Serena," he said quietly. He still wouldn't meet her eyes. He hadn't really looked at her since she'd changed. For some reason, that irritated Serena. She tried to focus on what he was saying. "The Federation," he continued. "Even if every human on this planet joined forces, we would still be like ants beneath a giant's foot. And they have men like Colley, soldiers even older than your father. Alone they are worth more than any army. We could never defeat them in a direct confrontation."

"Why are you telling me this, Rydian?"

Finally he lifted his head. His mouth was open as though to say something, but when he saw her, a strange look came over his face. The moment stretched out, before he swallowed and seemed to shake himself.

"Because I have a plan. But it's not something I can do alone."

Frowning, Serena lowered herself onto the sofa beside him. A tremor ran through her as his leg brushed against hers. "Tell me."

"That's just it," he breathed. "I can't."

"Why not?"

"Because I fear I have already said too much. Colley, his presence here is everything I feared—and everything I hoped for. We can't know exactly what he is capable of, but I know that some Lightmakers have the power to watch, to listen. So I need you to trust me. All of you, if this is going to succeed."

Serena swallowed. Rydian was asking a lot. But he *had* saved her. And her father...

"I need to see my father first."

"Of course." Rydian smiled. "We'll see him shortly. I gave the servants a dressing down last night, so he should have them tripping over themselves trying to please him by now."

She smiled. "Thank you, Rydian."

"It's nothing." He lowered his eyes. "The least I could do."

Taken by a sudden urge, Serena leaned across the table and gripped him by the shoulder. "No, Rydian. The least you could have done was nothing. And no one could have condemned you for it, after the way my people treated you."

Rydian puffed out his cheeks and then exhaled, but finally he nodded. Releasing him, Serena straightened.

"So...what now?"

"I've invited a few old friends to join us for a little talk. Come on, I had Brigg's prepare one of the meeting rooms for us."

Her hearts quickened at the mention of old friends. Had others amongst her people survived? But Rydian had already risen and was moving towards the door. She lingered, but only for a moment. What if they were other humans? She had regained some of her former confidence, but...she'd also spent six months bowing to their kind, suffering their cruel abuses. Even confronting the women last night had been too much for her wilted soul. Already she could feel herself trembling, but clenching her hands into fists, she forced those fears from her mind.

Father will be there. She rose. *And Rydian. You can do this.*

Quickening her step, she followed Rydian from the room and fell into step beside him. He cast another glance at her, his eyes seeming to linger, a questioning frown on his forehead, but she said nothing. Instead, she focused on maintaining a look of calm. At least her Light would not give her away. If there was one thing her people were skilled in, it was keeping their power concealed.

They wove their way through the tower, Rydian in the lead, until he stopped outside a familiar door. Serena shivered. Whether by instinct or design, the humans had chosen the very room the five Alfurian Princes had once met to discuss the governing of Talamh. Just the sight of the thick panelled doors had her cheeks growing pale with shameful memories of her bursting in to disrupt their meetings, to argue against their decisions. Little wonder they had never listened. She had been a child, raging against matters she couldn't begin to understand.

Serena wondered if any of the Princes or their heirs had escaped the conquest. Goma had fallen without resistance, but she knew little of what had passed in the other cities. Her stomach twisted at the thought of her brothers and sisters. She hadn't been particularly fond of the Princes and their bias against humanity, but many of the heirs had supported her. Had they also been thrown to the wolves, condemned to fight and die because of her failures?

She swallowed. Now she would sit with humans and discuss the future of Talamh. Just as the Princes once had. She didn't know what Rydian planned, but she hoped their fate would not be the same as their predecessors.

The doors hissed open and they stepped inside. Three people were already seated around the table within, but Serena only had eyes for one.

"Father!"

Forgetting all pretence of dignity, Serena threw herself across the room and swept Aiden Levaanton into a hug. A soft chuckling came from the former Prince as he hugged her back. It was a long moment before Serena recovered herself enough to pull back and look him up and down. She could hardly believe the change a night had made. His skin had regained its translucence and many of the wrinkles had left his face. He even felt more solid beneath her hands, rather than the ghost he had become in the cells beneath the arena.

But they could share in their relief later. For now Serena drew in her breath and did her best to regather her dignity as she turned to the others at the table. She recognised the hard-faced woman as Jasmine, Rydian's mother and the human who had been working with her father before the conquest. She seemed strangely empty to Serena's senses, until she noticed the Manus reader still embedded in her palm. It was still suppressing her power. Why had she not removed it?

Jasmine didn't acknowledge Serena's presence. Her eyes were distant, staring out the enormous window that took up an entire wall of the room. When it eventually became clear the older woman wasn't going to speak, the other human rose and offered his hand. From his size alone she knew him as the former gladiator, Bloodlust. He'd played a part in the distraction back when Rydian and Hazel had broken into the tower. It was said he'd killed many Alfur that day, and was celebrated as a hero amongst the humans of Talamh. She should hate him for that, but looking at the softness of his face, she couldn't bring herself to summon the emotion. He had only been fighting for his own people.

"Bloodlust," Serena greeted as she clasped his hand in the human gesture of greeting.

To her surprise, the man winced. "You can call my Johanas," he replied. "It's nice to finally meet in person, Ms Levaanton."

She smiled. "Serena, please."

A rumble came from her feet as an enormous cat rose from beneath the table. It took an effort of will for Serena not to throw herself back, but she had met Fatimah before. She nodded a greeting to the big cat.

"I'm sorry to call you all here under such short notice," Rydian began, and Serena quickly took a seat alongside her father. "I wish it could be under better circumstances. Now, if you're..."

Rydian trailed off as the mechanical doors behind him gave a hiss, then parted to permit the entrance of another guest. Serena frowned. She couldn't think who else Rydian might have invited.

Until the Queen of Goma strode through the open doors.

Hearts pounding hard in her chest, Serena stared at the woman who had overseen the systematic slaughter of her people these last six months, who had come to their prison cell every few months to torment them, who had brought about the fall of Talamh.

Hazel wore a sneer on her lips as she met Serena's gaze. A second woman had also followed her into the room.

"Gods below, Rydian, if I'd known you were inviting these scum, I'd have never stepped foot in the damned tower."

TWELVE

"Gods below, Rydian, if I'd known you were inviting these scum, I'd have never stepped foot in the damned tower."

Hazel's heart was pounding. She stood in the doorway of the conference room and did her best to *glare* at the Alfur who dared sit in her presence. The silence stretched out, until with a snort, Falcon stepped around her and swaggered into the room.

"Oy, Rydian dear, where's the drinks? Don't tell me you're throwing a party without any booze? Thought I taught you better than that!"

Without waiting for a reply, she stomped across to the table and took a seat. Her boots made an audible *clonk* as she leaned back in her chair and placed them on the table.

Hazel stood a moment longer, looking from one person to another. Johanas was about the only friendly face in the room. Jasmine was there as well, but there was no love lost between the two of them. Hazel's hatred was easy enough to understand—Jasmine was responsible for her brother's death.

The woman's animosity towards *her* was less comprehensible. It was like Jasmine hated her for saving her son's life—for saving all their lives, for that matter. Afterall, hadn't it been Hazel who had pulled the trigger and destroyed the Haze all those months ago? Rydian, Jasmine's own son, wouldn't be standing here right now if not for that.

Yet instead of praise, Hazel had earned only blame and hatred for that decision.

Her fists shook as she watched them, these people who had been her friends, her allies. Now they sat with the enemy, with those who had enslaved them, who had lied to and tormented their people for generations.

"Please, Hazel." That was Rydian. He held up his hands in a gesture of peace. "Take a seat, and I'll do my best to explain."

Hazel stared at the man. When he had come to her the night before, she'd been loath to accept his offer to meet. She'd expected him to make a gesture of peace or repentance for his actions in the arena. Instead he'd been all business.

Now she found he'd invited not only her sworn enemy, Jasmine—which was bad enough—but the Alfur along with her.

She would have turned and left then and there, if not for one thing.

Colley had already warned her Rydian might come. If she was truly an ally of the Federation, he had bid her accept any offer he might make, and report back to him.

So instead she clenched her jaw, met Rydian's eyes, and nodded.

But as she took a step towards the table, the young Alfur, Serena, came to her feet. Light lit beneath her translucent skin as she stepped between Hazel and her father, Aiden Levaanton. Gods, Hazel could hardly believe it. Rydian had actually given them Light! That was a hanging offence according to Federation regulations.

"Why don't you go on back to your tower, *Your Majesty?*" Serena hissed, her golden eyes meeting Hazel's. "You're not welcome here."

Hazel might have laughed at the threat implied by the Alfur's tone. Without a Manus reader, Alfur didn't have much in the way of overtly offensive capabilities with the Light. Sure, the Alfurian princess might have survived a few bouts in the arena against lesser foes, but Hazel was no amateur. And she had Light to spare now.

A sneer twisted her lips as she stared the Alfur down. "Is that so?" she whispered. "And what are you going to do about it, little Alfur?" Light congealed in her fingers, illuminating their faces with its eerie glow.

"Enough."

Rydian's voice was weary as he moved between them.

He glared at Hazel and she sneered back. What had he expected? That she would just go along and play nice with the enemy? Then he turned to Serena.

"I asked you to trust me, remember?"

Hazel frowned. What was Rydian up to? The pair stood frozen, eyes locked, and Hazel thought she glimpsed something in the face her foe...a familiarity? No. Gods, it was affection! She turned to Rydian, and saw the emotion reflected there as well. Her stomach twisted. How far down this traitorous path had her old friend gone?

Finally though, the Alfur exhaled. She turned without acknowledging Hazel and sat back down beside her father.

"Hazel, please." She flinched as she found Rydian's eyes on her once more. "Please, just take a seat. I need you all to listen."

"Why?" Now it was Jasmine's turn to interfere. The woman had finally decided to take part in the conversation it seemed. She glared at Hazel like she were evil incarnate. "I don't have any desire to share a table with that murderer."

That was almost too much for Hazel. Talk about the pot calling the kettle black. Her fists shook, the Light in her veins boiling beneath the surface. If not for Rydian, she would have struck the woman down then, and finally had justice for her brother. As it was, some remnant of respect still lingered in her heart for Rydian. It stayed her hand—just.

Instead, she held her head high and walked past Rydian, past Jasmine and Serena and the enormous cat curled up beneath Johanas's feet, all the way to the chair at the opposite end, where she took a seat for herself at the head of the table. It was only proper. She was the queen, after all.

Rydian watched her from the doorway, as though still trying to decide whether she could be trusted. Something in her eyes must have satisfied him though, for with a final nod, he took his chair at the other end of the table.

"Thank you all for coming," he began. "I understand there isn't much love lost amongst this group. I get it. Hate, it's...easier sometimes."

"Easier?" Hazel couldn't help herself. Her eyes turned to Jasmine. "You think it's easy, sitting at the same table as the woman who killed my brother? To dine with the woman who allowed our slavery to continue, knowing her actions are pardoned only because she's *your* mother? You think that's *easy?*"

"Easier than sitting in the same room as a genocidal maniac, I imagine," Jasmine muttered.

"*Enough!*" Rydian snapped. He drew in a breath before continuing. "We all hate each other, I get it—"

"I don't hate anyone." Johanas raised his hand, eyes lingering on Hazel.

Her stomach twisted and she refused to meet his gaze. If that was true, then where had he been these last six months, when she had needed him most? She said nothing though. Only pursed her lips and *glared* at the general table.

Until she looked into Johanas's eyes and saw the pain there. The sadness.

You could have visited.

They both could have visited. Why hadn't she gone down to the surface? She'd known where he was, after all. Was it because a part of her knew she could not look him in the eyes, after the things she'd done? Because some tiny voice within whispered that the things she did were wrong? Because she knew one look in her friend's eyes and she would no longer be able to tell the lies she'd whispered to herself these last six months?

"Can't say I'm much for hate either," Falcon chimed in, "but, and I really hate to be a nag, but I was promised booze..."

Rydian frowned. "I don't think I actually invited you, Falcon."

"Rude."

"Look, you can drink later—"

"Cause we have *business* to attend to, right?"

"Exactly."

"Great. So what's the plan then? Another revolution? Gonna gather all the escaped Alfur and lead them against the battleships outside? Maybe you're gonna go toe to toe with that general. I hear it was quite the match up in the arena, what with you sucker punching him and all. Probably should have finished him off then though. I've met some cold bastards in my time, but that man is glacial..." she trailed off—actually withered—beneath Rydian's gaze.

Hazel was impressed. There weren't many who could

silence Falcon with a look. Maybe Colley was right, and Rydian had grown during his time away. He'd certainly shown no power over the Goman champion when they'd been training under her.

Still, she didn't like where the woman was trying to steer them. Had Colley talked to Falcon as well? That would make sense—having two informants was a good way of ensuring no piece of intelligence was missed. But if that were true, Falcon was being far from subtle. She was practically *steering* Rydian into talk of treason.

"No," Rydian said, though whether he was refuting Falcon because her crassness given them away or because he really meant it, Hazel couldn't tell. "No more revolutions. That's how we got ourselves into this situation in the first place. We cannot fight the Federation."

"What then?" Jasmine demanded. "Don't tell me you think they'll change?" she sneered. "No son of mine could be that naïve."

Gods. Hazel looked from Jasmine to Rydian and saw the hurt in his eyes. The woman's bitterness knew no bounds.

"Then perhaps I am your son no longer," Rydian said, his voice like iron. "Though I suspect you are right and they will not change. Not when they are ruled by men who have lived for generations."

Hazel frowned. What was this?

Drawing in a breath, he met her eyes. "You have met the good general. Did you know he came to me last night? During our conversation, he revealed something...disturbing. He has lived more than five hundred years. No wonder they have become so fixed in their ways." Rydian paused then, drawing in a great breath. "But what is our excuse? We are young—you excluded, sorry Aiden. So why do we keep making the same mistakes of the past? If we want to move forward, we must find a way to live together, Alfur and human. No more rulers and the ruled. No more vengeance for the crimes of our ancestors. We need a new beginning, our species' working side by side, as our ancestors who first came to this planet once dreamed of."

There was silence in the room for a time, as those present contemplated his words. It was Aiden Levaanton who first broke the quiet.

"A fine dream, Rydian Holt," he said softly. "But men like Colley will never allow a world where Alfur walk free."

"You're right, of course," Rydian said after a pause. Clasping his hands behind his back, he stared down at the old Alfur. "You know him, don't you?"

"Yes," the old Alfur said simply, "how did you know?"

"You came up in our conversation last night," Rydian replied, turning his back on the room. "He made me an offer. He will spare Serena's life, if I place you into his custody by the end of the day."

"*What*—"

"I agree."

Hazel's head snapped around to stare at the elderly Alfur. Even his daughter had been silenced by his words.

"It is a good deal," the Alfur's voice was soft now, considered. Serena sat tense at his side, fingers gripping the table so tight Hazel thought the steel might bend. "I would gladly give my life, that my daughter's might continue."

"No," Serena growled. Her eyes turned on Rydian. "You asked me to trust you, but this, this...I won't let you do this."

"He cannot save me from this enemy, my daughter," Aiden said. "I had hoped this was a wrath we might yet escape. That our enemies might perish while we remained safe within the Haze. Alas, fate was not so kind. Saxon Colley will have my life one way or another."

"Why does he hate you so?" Rydian murmured.

The Alfur turned its golden eyes on Rydian. "Because his daughter chose to come with me. Because I took her from him. Because I am responsible for her death."

Rydian clenched his jaw. "He said something similar."

Hazel bunched her fists in her pockets and wished she could close them around the old Alfur's throat. So *that* was why Colley was willing to go to such lengths to kill Aiden Levaanton. She could understand that rage, after what Jasmine had done to her brother. But already the arrogant little Alfur was speaking again.

"...don't care, I won't let you do it."

"I know," Rydian said softly. And she saw it. The look in his eyes. He *liked* her. Bastard! "Which means we have the day to prepare."

Hazel could hardly believe what she was hearing.

"Have you lost your mind, Rydian?" she cried. "Colley will *destroy* you. Didn't you can't fight the Federation?"

"You're right, of course," he said with a sigh. "I don't have that power. I cannot protect everyone in the galaxy. And I can't change it. But a wise man once told me to focus on what I *can* change. And maybe, just maybe, there's a way to save Talamh."

"What?"

Rydian met Hazel's gaze down the length of the table. "True freedom," he continued. "For humanity *and* the Alfur. A world where we live side by side as equals."

"The Federation—"

"The Federation can keep their cursed heavens. Talamh is *ours*."

Hazel's heart lurched. "You don't mean that, Rydian."

He turned from her then, and looked again to the Alfurian girl. And in that gesture, Hazel knew his mind was set. She could not save him.

"I've already made my decision, Hazel."

She bowed her head. Inwardly, her heart was racing, her stomach twisting in agony. She couldn't keep this from Colley. If she said nothing, Falcon would. And then she would be in line for the gibbet with the other traitors.

"Then I cannot protect you, Rydian," she whispered.

"What?"

Across the table, Falcon began to laugh. Even Hazel frowned, lifting her head to stare. What had become of the woman?

A shadow fell across the window. They all turned to

see what manner of creature or ship had flown so close to the tower.

At that moment, the glass *imploded*.

And a dozen soldiers came crashing through to land in their midst.

THIRTEEN

RYDIAN ONLY HAD SECONDS TO REACT AS THE soldiers came smashing through the window. How hadn't he sensed their presence? Colley must have been suppressing their aura somehow. Damnit. Rydian hadn't even known that was a possibility.

"Everyone grab a hold of me!" He screamed as the soldiers raised their hands and he felt the shimmering of Light gathering for an attack. He could probably take them, but any fighting in this packed space was bound to end in collateral damage.

Serena was fastest, grasping him with one hand and her father with the other. The warmth of Fatimah's fur brushed against his legs from beneath the table. Then his heart was racing as he turned for his mother. Her eyes were wide as they met his gaze, and he saw the pain there. She hadn't believed he was actually working against the Federation, not really. Now she knew it.

And so Jasmine Holt turned towards the soldiers.

Rydian saw what she was about to do and opened his mouth to scream—but the words never left his mouth.

Instead, Johanas's shoulder careened into Jasmine. She cried out as the collision sent her stumbling away from the soldiers and into Rydian's waiting hands.

"Go, Rydian!" Johanas's cry echoed through the room.

Then with a blaze of brilliance, Johanas called upon his Light. By its burning power, he turned and charged the soldiers.

"Johanas!" he cried, but there was no pulling him back now. He had already engaged with the soldiers, providing Rydian with the cover he needed to flee.

He watched his friend for a second, before his eyes darted to the other end of the table, where Hazel had half-risen from her seat.

"Rydian, don't—" she began.

Light swallowed them.

He couldn't take them far, not with so many. At least he'd confirmed his suspicions—the man *could* listen in on them, if not their minds, their words at least. Rydian had hoped for a more moderated reaction, but he'd obviously underestimated the general's hatred for Aiden Levaanton.

He hadn't wanted to make his move so soon, but the general left him with no choice. If he took them into the city, they'd never make it back to the tower, and besides, that was where they would be expected to flee.

So instead, Rydian directed his power into a downwards spiral, down to the site of disaster from so many months ago, to a location he hoped the general would never think to look for them.

The air crackled and someone screamed as they crashed through reality and landed in the control room buried deep in the basement of the Levaanton tower. The room that had once controlled the Haze around the planet.

Rydian's knees gave out as they landed. He collapsed to the floor, gasping for breath, even as he replayed those final moments in the room over and over in his mind. Of Johanas, screaming, blazing with power, charging the soldiers. And of Hazel, the rage he'd seen in her eyes as they fled...

...they were his friends. They always would be. But he'd left them behind. He clenched his eyes closed, heart palpitating. Hazel had always been hard, but before that had only been a façade, a sharpness she used to hide the kindness at her core. Now that kindness had been smothered, and Rydian could not think of the words he needed to bring it back, to restore the Hazel he'd known.

And Johanas...poor, gentle Johanas. Once again forced to fight. He reached out for his friend's Light and found it almost immediately, though it was already guttering beneath the onslaught of others in the room.

As he watched, a brilliance appeared, one he recognised as General Colley. In an instant, his power overwhelmed Johanas, though to Rydian's relief, his friend was not entirely snuffed out. He quickly withdrew his senses before the general detected him.

His stomach twisted, but there was nothing he could do for his friend. Not yet. Talamh needed him.

"Rydian, why have you brought us here?"

He looked around at Serena's question, but before Rydian could answer, the elder Alfur gripped him suddenly by the arm.

"He's seeking us," Aiden hissed, and for the first time, Rydian saw some emotion in the elder Alfur's eyes. Fear. "Quickly, Rydian, lend me your strength. I can hide us, for a time at least, from his view."

Rydian swallowed at the desperation in the man's voice. A second later he too felt the probing mind sweeping outwards from the tower above. It boiled with Colley's rage. If the general found them here, there would be no escaping a second time. His training hadn't mentioned anything like what Aiden suggested. He hesitated only a second before allowing his Light to flow into the Alfurian Prince.

The man jolted at the surge of power, his frail body growing tense, his eyes distant. Rydian watched as the power swept through the Alfur's channels, momentarily overwhelming, before the famous Alfurian control reinstated itself. Without a Manus reader, Aiden could do little to affect the environment without himself, so instead he reached for Rydian, their powers mingling...

And Rydian *saw*. Saw what he needed to do. Light rippled between himself and Aiden. Grasping it, he directed it *outwards*, pushing it passed the barrier of his flesh, just as he did when he formed weapons or energy blasts. But instead of the great quantities used in such attacks, now he needed only a tiny measure, a whisper that swept from him, shifting outwards to cover the chamber—then even further, pushing outwards until the entire basement was consumed by the pulse of power.

Rydian shivered as he withdrew his mind back to his body and felt how the room had changed. It wasn't a physical sensation, so much as a...a silence of the mind. All those voices he'd once heard whispering, buzzing, *screaming* over the surface of the planet were cut off, as though their connection through the Light had been severed.

A long exhalation came from the elder Alfur. He slumped against Rydian. "That was...well done, Rydian Holt," Aiden Levaanton breathed. Concern showed on Serena's face and she moved towards them, but Aiden waved her off and straightened. "You are a better man that I had thought possible from your kind." His eyes dipped. "It...shames me to admit, but...I fear my daughter was right, all those months ago. If we had only listened, perhaps...but no, we cannot alter what has been." The Alfur's words trailed off in a sigh.

Rydian's stomach twisted. He understood this was probably as close to an apology as he would ever get from the proud Prince. The words should have been affirming, to know their former overlords had finally been made to see the folly of their ways, but instead they grated, the knowledge they came too late for so many a pain in Rydian's core.

But anger would not help him or Talamh now. The Prince was right—they could not change the past.

"Thank you for that, Aiden," he said.

He glanced around at his companions. Aiden. Serena. Jasmine. And a rumble from his side, Fatimah. Hazel and Johanas were already lost to him, and he had not seen what had become of Falcon. He hoped this would be enough.

"Why have you brought us here, son?" His mother whispered. Her eyes were on the machines that dominated one wall of the room.

Rydian drew in a breath and met his mother's eyes. "Because this is the place where it all began. Where you turned against your own people. Where Hazel brought the Federation down upon us. It only seems right that this is where it ends."

Her eyes widened, but it was Serena who spoke what they were all thinking. "You want to use the Haze against them."

His heartbeat slowed as he looked at the Alfur. She stood before the bank of machines, staring at the black screens that had once captured images from all across the galaxy. Images of her own people, suffering, dying by the hands of humanity.

Beneath the Federation, he reminded himself. *Humanity, we can be better, even if...if we cannot save them all.*

Serena's golden eyes met his. "That's your plan, isn't it? That's why you saved us? So we could repair it?"

Rydian swallowed the lump in his throat. "I..." he trailed off. What more could he say?

Serena turned to her father. "Can you?"

Frowning, Aiden wandered across to the machines. To Rydian's eye they mostly seemed intact—but then he knew little of how Alfurian technology functioned—any technology, for that matter. The old Alfur's gaze passed over the blank screens, lingering on a few that had been smashed by Hazel all that time ago. Broken panels revealed a mess of wire and boards of dull lights within. All of it was far beyond Rydian's comprehension.

"Perhaps," the older Alfur murmured, then turned, "though it would be easier with your aid, Ms Holt."

His mother frowned, but crossing her arms, she moved to join the Alfur. "The damage doesn't seem as bad as I feared," she said after a few minutes inspecting the mechanisms. "Most of this is on the monitoring equipment, rather than the controls connecting with the satellite."

"Satellite?" Serena questioned.

"These computers only form a small function in the entire array. Our cities were structured so as to draw residual Light from the surrounding environments, then distribute it around the planet for maximum efficacy. It should still work, though the amount of power taken from the human population is likely to have dropped substantially without the Manus readers to augment the efficiency."

Rydian pursed his lips at that piece of news. He'd already known the Alfur had been using the devices to siphon off their Light, but the truth didn't get any easier with repetition. But he did not interrupt the man's explanation.

"The control system has been moved many times in the past, disguised as various functions amongst the human population. Only recently were such extreme measures needed to protect it that we moved it into our tower itself."

"How does it transform all that Light into the Haze though?" Rydian asked. The floating miasma of pain and suffering that was the Haze had been the antithesis of the Light. He couldn't understand how one could have created the other.

"Simple. The towers in each city collect and magnify the signal from all that Light, then transmit it to the satellite, Belaaros."

Belaaros... "Wait, you mean?" Belaaros was one of the twin moons that orbited Talamh.

"It is a construct we created as part of our great experiment. We deconstructed the galactic fleet we appropriated from the Federation and put it to another use."

"That's...insane."

"And yet it worked. Belaaros receives the transmissions from each of the five cities, and then broadcasts them back across the planet. Or at least, it did."

"And that..."

"...amplifies the mental energies of every Light imbued being on the planet, damaging their cognitive functions over time, and eventually driving them—"

"To madness," Rydian finished for the Alfur. He swallowed, looking from his mother to the Alfur. "So this terminal, it controls all of this? And you believe you can repair it?"

The two shared a look, then nodded.

"Good," he breathed.

"Rydian," Serena had remained quiet all this time, but when he turned to her, he found the younger Alfur's golden eyes fixed on him. "This...plan, you know if the Haze is restored...it would destroy you."

Rydian pursed his lips. "I understand the risks."

"But your own people here, they no longer wear their Manus readers. It would—"

"I said I understand," Rydian interrupted.

She stared at him for a long moment. He could see the question in her eyes, but even now he dared not tell her the full extent of his plans. They might be protected for now, but the more who knew, the greater the chance his plan fell into the wrong hands. Though...he glanced at Aiden. If what the Alfur said was true, then maybe, just maybe, Rydian's plan might succeed.

"What's this all about, Rydian?" she said at last. "You said you wanted human and Alfur to work side by side. This will destroy your own people, everyone on Talamh."

"I know, Serena," Rydian replied. "I need you to trust me one more time."

She pursed her lips, but in the end, she nodded. He turned to his mother, who was just straightening from a more thorough inspection of the machinery.

"I think we can use parts from the other machines to make the repairs. If we could have returned here, we could have repaired it long ago. Not that it would have done much good, once the Federation found us..." Her lips tightened and Rydian knew she was thinking about Hazel.

He nodded. He didn't ask why she wasn't concerned about the humans of Talamh. His mother had decided long ago that humanity had no worth. He could only hope that one day, Talamh would show her the error in her judgement

"Do what you can."

"There's something else," Aiden interrupted. He was standing at another of the machines, the ones that had projected the images from the other planets conquered by the Federation. "Before we pull these apart, there is something I must retrieve."

Rydian's stomach twisted. He thought he knew what the Alfurian prince wanted. "We can't save everyone, Aiden," he said. "Trying to contact Alfur from other planets will warn the Federation what we're up too."

The old Alfur regarded him. "I am not a fool, Rydian Holt," he said at last. "But it is not that. There is an old... record I think may help us."

"I'm not sure..." Rydian began, but his mother was already waving a hand.

"Here, Aiden, that one seems to be untouched." She pointed a finger without even lifting her head from the machine she had begun working on. "I shouldn't need anything from it for my repairs. You're welcome to search for whatever you want."

The Alfur nodded and sat himself at the device Jasmine indicated. Rydian lingered a moment, but there was nothing else he could do here. At least, not for now. There was a final modification they would need, but he needed to speak with Aiden about that. Privately. And then...

...well, then they would discover just what kind of man he was.

FOURTEEN

JOHANAS ROSE SLOWLY FROM THE PIT THE OTHER man's Light had thrown him into. Once, when he'd used the Light for violence, he had gloried in the power it had given him, in the sense of invincibility. But that had been the wasting effects of the Haze, and when the slaughter was done, Johanas had felt only a forlorn sense of loss.

This time when he'd attacked the soldiers, there had been no rush of glory, no ecstasy as the power burst from him to cut down one man, then another. He'd felt the pain, the regret of his violence, even as his foes had fallen.

So he'd embraced the appearance of the older man. General Colley, Rydian had named him. He had stepped from nowhere in the same instant Rydian and the others disappeared. At least Johanas had managed that much, with his bloodshed.

The general had not shared his sentiment. Johanas had had only a moment to look upon the man before the full force of his rage struck. A blast of Light, an all-consuming sensation of oppression, and then he'd been falling, his consciousness crushed to a flickering spark, his mind...consumed.

Truth was, he'd embraced that darkness, that opening of the abyss. Anything to escape the weight of guilt that came when he killed, to finally pay the price for his evil.

He'd thought it done. That the general had struck Johanas a mortal blow. Now he realised his error, that even in his rage, this man he and his friend faced was no mortal foe, capable of such a basic error. He had neutralised the threat Johanas posed, but held him to life, no doubt for later questioning.

That was at the forefront of Johanas's mind when he finally blinked awake. The light in the room was bright—bright enough that for a second he could not see. A shadow shifted in the white. So he was not alone. Johanas clenched his fists, only to find them bound by cuffs of fiery Light. There would be no breaking those bonds, though he still tested his strength against them, and found himself wanting.

"A precautionary measure," a voice nearby said. "I'm sure you understand."

Johanas gritted his teeth and tried to will the fog from his vision. Bit by bit, the stars of brightness faded, until he found himself looking up into the face of an older man. He recognised the general from the brief glimpse he'd gotten during the battle, though the man was no longer lit by the glow of his own power.

"General Colley, I presume?"

A smile touched the man's lips. "And they tell me you went by Bloodlust, during your arena days."

"It is Johanas now."

"So I understand. Though, I am not sure what could motivate a man to surrender such a noble name."

"Noble?" Johanas stared in disbelief. "There was nothing noble about the blood shed by my blade, General. Only shame, that I didn't have the courage to refuse."

"I see."

The general crossed the room and crouched down where Johanas lay. Now his vision had returned, he realised they were still in the conference room. The steel table lay nearby, twisted and broken by a ricochet of Light from the battle. And beyond...Johanas's stomach twisted when he saw the bodies. The men he had struck down still lay where they had fallen.

"And what of them, Johanas?" the general continued. "If the gladiator within lives no more, why do these sorry souls lie dead on your floor?"

Johanas squeezed his eyes shut. His heart pounded in his chest. He tried to reach out through the Light for his friends, for anyone, but the cuffs muted his power and he found only silence.

"A shame, to see such potential fighting for the enemy."

"Maybe I do not see them as the enemy," Johanas breathed. Opening his eyes, he fixed them on the general. He couldn't show weakness here.

"Then you would be a fool. I have heard your story, Johanas. How the Alfur judged your size as proof of your violent nature. How they sent you to the arena to fight and kill. Do you truly think a species of such cruelty deserves to stand beside us as equals?"

He could have laughed at that. The hypocrisy was too great. "How can you not?"

The general smirked. "I suppose humanity is not without its cruelties. But believe me when I say it is better that we control the galaxy, than the Alfur."

"Why does anyone need to control the galaxy?"

"The argument of a child. It is the rule of the universe, that the strong govern the weak." He leaned forward, so that they were eye to eye. "Would you like to know a secret, Bloodlust?"

"Not particularly. My father always said history is told by the victor."

"A wise man. Still, perhaps I can enlighten you somewhat to the actions of our Federation. You see, humanity has not always ruled the known universe. When we first ventured away from our home world, out into the grand expanse of space, we knew little of the universe and the Light. But as we expanded across galaxies, colonising planets and exploring the vast beauties of existence, we began to encounter...abnormalities."

Johanas frowned but said nothing, and the general continued.

"Empty worlds. Filled with noble cities, the remains of great civilisations. Yet their peoples had vanished. And amongst the sentient species we encountered, whispers. Rumours of demons that haunted the outermost reaches of the galaxy. We thought little of them—until one day, our forces returned to a colonised world, and met the demons for ourselves."

"The Alfur?"

"Ay, the Alfur," Colley confirmed. "They had come upon the colony while our forces were absent. We did not know what Light was, back then, but the Alfur did. They had evolved to *consume* it. They considered themselves the apex predator of the galaxy. And in our species, with all the unknown Light imbued in our lifeforce, they had found the perfect prey. Tell me, Bloodlust, did you have tales of vampires on this planet?"

Johanas shook his head, and the general pursed his lips. "No, I suppose that is a tale they would have suppressed above all others." Reaching into his pocket, the general drew out a metallic device. A Manus reader. "You see, back then the Alfur did not have these machines. But there are other ways to take someone's Light. They didn't kill our people, but when the Alfur consumed their power, it changed them. Took...*something* from them." His eyes flickered, becoming haunted. "They'd been keeping the humans in prison camps, to feed upon at their leisure. They were a small group, else I fear we would have never driven them from such a feast."

Silence fell over the room, cut only by the swirling of the wind outside the broken window. Johanas watched the general's face and saw the horror there, and wondered...

"Their minds were gone," the man said suddenly. "We thought we'd saved them, but what the Alfur left...they could still function. Walk and eat and drink. But there was nothing left of the people they'd been. Whatever process the Alfur had used to drain their Light had turned them into the walking dead."

Despite himself, Johanas shivered, imagining such an emptiness.

Abruptly, the general straightened, his face regaining its emotionless expression. "After that, we fought a decades long war to put the Alfur in their place."

"And how long ago was this?"

"Centuries."

"You don't think they could have changed? That they might be worthy of a little dignity?"

"Perhaps that is what your friend thinks," the general replied. "That they deserve a second chance. Yet they had that here, and what did they do? Once more they enslaved us, used their power and technology to cripple us. You know what they're capable of. So tell me where Rydian has taken them, and I will do all in my power to ensure your friend does not come to any harm."

Johanas swallowed. The general's words were compelling, and yet...

...and yet he had seen the cruelty humanity was capable of. Could he honestly say the galaxy was any better under their rule, than the Alfur's?

"I'm sorry. I don't know where he has gone, what he has planned."

"Very well," Colley said as he rose. His eyes drifted to the broken window. "Then I am afraid I cannot protect either of you from what is to come."

"Surely the all-powerful Federation cannot feel threatened by one little human."

"One powerful human, and a pair of Alfur of the royal bloodlines," Colley rebuked, his voice strangely gentle as he sighed. "I came here for vengeance. I did not expect to find myself confronted by open rebellion." He rose, towering over Johanas. "I fear your friend has forced my hand. I must contact command and re-evaluate our options with his planet. It seems those who argued for extermination may have had the right of it after all."

Johanas's head jerked up. "What? You wouldn't—there are hundreds of millions here—"

"Ay, and I had hoped Aiden Levaanton would die by my own hand," the general murmured. "But the Federation must be protected, whatever the cost." He eyed Johanas. "Think about that, while you wait here. Perhaps you will reconsider your position."

With that he turned and strode from the room.

FIFTEEN

Serena moved carefully through the winding corridors, into the dark depths of her family tower. There was no Light illuminating these hallways, no humming of the inner machinery, but she remained on the alert for intruders. The stairwell leading up to the occupied floors of the tower was nearby, and while they were protected from unseen eyes, there was nothing to stop a curious human from venturing down to this abandoned sublevel.

Their only light came from Rydian. His soft footsteps followed her through the winding hallways. They had left Jasmine and her father to work while they searched for a supply of Manus readers. Her father claimed some had been in storage down here when the conquest happened. Rydian hadn't explained the rest of his plan with the Haze, but he agreed Manus readers might prove useful. Serena hoped so. If the Haze was activated while Rydian remained unprotected...

For some reason, the thought had her insides tying themselves in knots. She cast a glance over her shoulder at him, but Rydian's eyes were distant, his mind clearly elsewhere. She felt a pang of guilt. If not for her, Rydian wouldn't be in this position. Under the Federation, he could have had anything he wanted. Power, fame, riches. Instead he was once more fighting for his life—and the lives of a people who until six months ago had viewed him as little more than a violent animal.

A rumble came from her side and she glanced down as Fatimah's bulk rubbed against her leg. A wry smile touched her lips. She supposed they *had* been wrong on even that count. Without the Haze to hinder them, it seemed many of the animals on Talamh were quite sentient.

Her smile was short lived. Truly, her people didn't deserve such kindness, after everything they'd done. By rights, Rydian should have turned his back on the Alfur the second their empire crumbled...

Her hearts fluttered as Rydian blinked, his eyes suddenly meeting hers. She quickly looked around—and spied a door the same as all the others they'd passed. She decided it looked promising.

"Let's try this one!" she said, her voice not at all shrill for an Alfur. Why was she so flustered? "This symbol means storage," she continued, pointing to a star beside the door. Most of the walls down here were unadorned, being recent additions to the tower, but at least the coding system had been included. "Hopefully no one has been down here yet and raided the equipment."

"I doubt it. The Federation have been reluctant to commit resources to Talamh," Rydian mused.

Pushing open the door, Serena allowed Rydian to take the lead. She could have generated some Light through her own skin, but it was a wasteful way to brighten a room. And without a Manus reader she couldn't manifest it as Rydian had, in a little ball of brilliance that hung in his hand. Another reason she hoped this mission would be successful.

Inside they found a room filled with shelves, each stacked with containers marked and categorised with the language of her people. That would cut down on time. Walking along the shelves, she searched the boxes. Most contained components she recognised as parts for the Manus readers, but Serena wasn't an engineer. Of the Alfurian heirs on Talamh, Willis had been the only one with a mind for technology. But he...

She forced the thought from her mind. They didn't know what had become of the other cities, the other Princes and their heirs. Maybe Willis and others still lived.

She paused at another box with parts she recognised. Her father could possibly put a Manus reader together, if she could find all the parts they needed. She pursed her lips. No, time was not on their side, and they needed one for Rydian as well.

Finally she saw the symbol she'd hoped for. Relief flooded her Light channels as she lifted the container from its shelf and saw the Manus readers rolling around in the bottom. A little thrill of excitement touched her. Finally, she would no longer be helpless. Finally, she would have her power back.

There were only half a dozen of the devices, but it was better than nothing. Not long ago, they'd had entire factories dedicated to the manufacture of Manus readers, but those had all been destroyed once the humans of Talamh learned what the devices had really been for. These might be the only ones left on the planet.

Most were marked as human devices—Manus readers designed to suppress the Light of the human it was fitted too. There was only one marked for an Alfur. But one was all she needed. Rydian raised an eyebrow as she drew it out and clutched it tight in her hand.

"Find what you were looking for?"

She nodded, showing him the container with the remaining devices. "These are the ones you and your friends will need." Her eyes fell to the one she held. "This...this one's for me."

A frown creased Rydian's forehead. "Can you use it...I mean, without..." He gestured to her hand.

Serena held her hand up to the light. An ugly, jagged scar had been left where the humans had torn out her Manus reader. A reminder of the torments she'd suffered these last six months. Starved of Light, she couldn't even accelerate its healing. On cold nights, she still felt the pain of its removal in the bones of her hand.

She clenched her fist around the device. They had

taken so much from her, the Federation, but the Manus reader was the worst of it. Without the device, she'd felt as though a part of her was missing, that she had been cut off from the world, from her connection to the Light.

Now she could have it all back.

"I need a knife," she breathed, turning her eyes on Rydian.

"You can't be serious?"

"I'm tired of being helpless, Rydian. Even with the Light you gave me, I'm no good to you, not if it comes to a fight. But with this, maybe, just maybe, having my powers back will even the playing field."

He pursed his lips. She could see the doubt in his eyes, but at last he nodded. "I can understand that."

Her hearts fluttered. "Thank you."

She spied a table and chairs in the corner of the storage room, probably used for sorting through components. Carrying the container of Manus readers with her, Serena crossed to the table and took a seat. When Rydian sat in the chair beside her, she held out her hand. He hesitated before taking it. She shivered at the warmth of his fingers against her skin.

"Are you sure?"

"I'm sure. I can heal, remember, so long as you lend me the Light."

Rydian puffed out his cheeks. "Okay then."

Exhaling, he studied her hand closely, then reached out with his other. Light sparked between his fingers before expanding to form a knife. Serena suppressed a pang of jealously. Even at the height of her powers, she couldn't achieve such a solid manifestation of Light. It was excessively wasteful, of course; humans lacked the finesse of the Alfur, after all. That had been one of the many arguments her father and the other Princes used to justify the need for their dominion over the 'barbaric' humans.

She clenched her teeth as Rydian leaned forward with the knife, eying the scar where reader had been.

"Wait!"

He froze. Drawing in a breath, Serena stilled the racing of her hearts. She placed the Manus reader on the table where she would not drop it. Then she locked eyes with Rydian.

"Now."

He didn't hesitate. The knife plunged down and icy fire swallowed Serena's hand. It took all her courage not to scream—and even then, a whimper slipped from her lips. Clenching her teeth so hard she feared they might crack, Serena fumbled for the Manus Reader with her good hand, but she was shaking so badly she couldn't even lift it. Rydian took it from her fingers.

"Here," he said gently.

She nodded, hoping he knew what he was doing. Her entire body was coiled like a spring. Blood dripped from her hand as Rydian dismissed the dagger and lifted the device carefully between his fingers. She gritted her teeth. Normally this was done while a patient was anesthetised. At least they didn't need to shift any bones or nerves or veins—that work had already been done when Serena received her first reader as a child.

So she clung to the table with her good hand, stars dancing before her eyes, and did her best not to pass out. All Rydian need to do now was...

And it was done. Serena exhaled slowly. She'd felt it, the moment the device aligned with her Light channels. A sudden *rightness*. Energy rippled through her arm, spreading through her body, tingling as it went. Her connection with the world, missing for so many months, came rushing back, like a lost limb miraculously restored.

Light bloomed deep within the Manus reader, in the crystal at its core. Even in the grips of agony, Serena breathed easier. Teeth clenched, she wrapped her fingers around the torn flesh. The pain disrupted her concentration and she struggled to reach for the Light she needed to heal—

Serena gasped as Light *flooded* her in a rush of brilliance. She clutched at it, drawing it into the wound, feeding it to the torn flesh and broken sinews, and some of her pain receded. Even for her, such a wound might have taken hours to heal with Light, but Serena could feel Rydian's hand on her arm, the enormity of his power. It came to her like an endless flood. So she poured it recklessly into the wound and watched the tissue knit itself back together around her new Manus reader.

Finally it was done. She sagged in her chair, gasping with sudden exhaustion. Red flashed at the edges of her vision and the world spun. Before she knew what was happening, Serena felt herself toppling.

Strong arms caught her before she could fall. Eyes scrunched closed, she struggled to stop the spinning, to resist the nausea that came with overusing Light. She'd pushed herself too far, between the pain and the rapid healing. But slowly, she felt the fluctuations in the Light fade, regulate. The Manus reader helped with that, helped to better her senses, to add another level of finesse to her control.

When Serena finally opened her eyes again, Rydian was staring down at her. A smile touched her lips as she saw his face, the concern in his eyes...

...without thinking, she reached up and cupped his cheek, pulling him down. He didn't resist as their lips met. If the fire of his Light had been exhilarating, it was nothing to the heat shared between them now, to the sudden racing of her hearts, the gasping of their mingled breaths.

Then Rydian was pulling away, though his eyes never left hers. "We don't have to do this...you..."

"I know."

Serena smiled as she kissed him again.

SIXTEEN

Hazel paced the landing dock of the arena, hands clasped behind her back, head down, teeth clenched. Damnit, why was everyone such *idiots!* Couldn't they see that the Alfur were manipulating them? That the damned Prince and his daughter didn't give a damn whether Rydian and the others lived or died, so long as *they* survived.

She should have dealt with them months ago. Thrown them into one of the wolf pack matches, where no one survived.

Instead she'd allowed her own gratification blind her to the threat. She'd enjoyed watching Serena fight for her life. Just as *she* had been forced to fight. And now...

...now Rydian was at large. He of all people should have known better. Him and his insane plans. And he'd dragged the others down with him. Jasmine she could not have cared less for, but Johanas...her friend had sacrificed his own freedom so the others could escape. General Curtis was not likely to look past that, even if he cooperated, which wasn't exactly likely.

Even Falcon had vanished in the confusion. Hazel hadn't seen what had become of the former champion, but could only assume she too had abandoned her.

Damn them all to the heavens.

Gritting her teeth, Hazel cast an impatient glance at the starship. She'd been pulled away from the Levaanton tower by other duties. She was loathe to leave Johanas alone with the general, but he'd been unconscious when she'd left. Hopefully he would not wake until her return.

In the meantime, a steady stream of fresh prisoners stomped down the ramp of the ship into the hanger bay of the arena. There, her personal guards shepherded them into the corridor and down to the cells. Normally there would be soldiers on duty to oversee such a task, but those had been commandeered by the general when he'd decided to throw off his cloak of anonymity. Thanks to Johanas, most of them were now recovering in hospital beds, so she'd been forced to bring in her own guards to help with the transfer. A prison break of criminal Alfur was the last thing she needed right now.

She watched as the last prisoner disembarked, one finger tapping impatiently against her elbow. The Alfur from beyond Talamh certainly made a wretched image. Their skin was cracked and broken, their silver eyes the only spot of brightness in the sunken pits of their faces.

Most moved with their heads bowed, their bare feet stumbling on the bricked surface.

Broken, defeated, they followed one another down into the depths of the arena with hardly a whimper. In truth, it was hard to reconcile these pitiful things with the creatures that had ruled over Talamh her entire life. These Alfur were so pathetic, it was difficult to hate them.

Serena and Aiden though...

How could Rydian have chosen to protect them? Before she'd destroyed the Haze, they had been willing to *kill* him. To strike him down to bury their dirty little secret. It had been *Hazel* who had stopped them, who had saved Rydian's godsdamn life.

How had she become the bad guy?

A cry came from nearby as one of the Alfurian prisoners stumbled and fell out of line. A guard stepped in immediately to place himself between her and the creature, but she waved him aside. These Alfur were so starved, they were no threat to her.

The individual was a female of the species. Their eyes met as it looked up, before stretching out a pleading hand.

"Light, please..." it rasped.

Despite herself, Hazel's stomach twisted. She started to raise a hand before she caught herself. She wasn't Rydian, disobeying Federation rules left and right and expecting to be forgiven. Besides, wretched or no, these creatures were still the enemy. Colley had told her the story, the tale of their vampiric past...

Thwack.

She flinched as the guard stepped forward at the Alfur's gesture and backhanded it across the face. The blow sent the creature toppling backwards, though it barely gave a whimper. Grasping it by an arm, the guard dragged the Alfur back into line and then forced her to her feet.

Hazel watched in silence after that, unable to speak, until the last of the Alfurian prisoners were led into the depths. Only then did she blink and come back to herself. The last of her guards had returned, the prisoners safely locked away. It was time she returned to the tower and found out what Colley planned to do next.

That thought was enough to jolt Hazel back to herself. Needles pricked at her scalp as she turned her eyes to the sky. Rydian, Jasmine, Johanas, none of them seemed to realise just how precarious their situation was here on Talamh. Colley had an entire star fleet at his command. If he truly felt they posed a threat, he would obliterate the planet without hesitation.

Her hands were trembling as she boarded the smaller ship to take her back to the tower. The pilot turned in his seat as she entered with her guard. He was another off-worlder and had been ordered to remain in the ship, but from his position in the cockpit he must have seen the prisoners being unloaded. She took the co-pilot seat beside him while her guards gripped the straps on the walls of the hold. It was only a short flight, but you never knew what might happen in the air.

"You have Alfur on your planet, Captain Briggs?" she

asked the man, curious despite herself about the galaxy. As far as she knew, Rydian was the only human from Talamh so far to experience that world.

"Not my planet, no," he replied.

Hazel pursed her lips. "I thought they were everywhere."

"They are a useful...tool for some." He paused. "I was told this planet had a somewhat...unique population of Alfur."

"Were you now?" This was the captain who had piloted the ship Rydian had arrived on. It didn't take much imagination to figure out who might have told him about their Alfur.

The captain chuckled. "Don't worry, I won't be saying anything to anyone. I like my head on my shoulders." He paused and she saw his eyes were on the towers rising ahead of them. "I spoke with the old one actually, just this morning. Fascinating, hearing his regrets. A shame our species seem destined to forever be enemies. Seems like we could learn a lot from one another."

Hazel sighed but did not answer. This, she supposed, was why the Federation hadn't wanted their own people interacting with Talamh. Gods damn Rydian. Was he determined to ruin everything for them?

"Look at all that green," the pilot continued. They were high now, approaching the docking bay for the Levaanton tower, but she saw his eyes were on the distant jungles. "On my planet, there's hardly a patch of green across the entire surface. Apart from the greenhouses, of course."

Hazel frowned. She'd always hated the jungle, but then, she'd been taken there to be trained as a gladiator. Back then, it had been filled with deadly, Haze-maddened beasts. She'd heard it had changed since, that it had become a more forgiving place, but the new queen no longer had time to wander amongst the trees. But...

"Have you seen the ocean?" she asked, surprising herself.

"Not here. I imagine it must be beautiful. Ours is toxic and brown." He sighed and cast a glance behind them, as though to check on the guards, but they would hear little of their conversation over the whirring of engines from the back of the ship. "That's the thing. The Federation recognises us only for the resources we provide. There is no time for beauty, or freedom, in their world." His cheeks wrinkled in a sad smile. "Something to think about, no doubt."

The conversation died after that, as the captain brought them around to the docking bay. But not before Hazel found herself glancing again at the vast jungle, her mind returning to that distant shoreline, the gentle rumble of water as it lapped against the sands.

The corridors of the Levaanton tower were empty as Hazel strode their lengths. She marked the time through the enormous windows, where the sun was falling rapidly towards the horizon. Another day almost done, and the general still did not have his vengeance. How long could this last? She didn't want to find out what the man was capable of when aggravated.

Colley found Hazel before she found him. She yelped as he materialised in front of her, seemingly stepping out of empty air.

"Gods," she gasped. "Someone needs to show me how to do that someday."

The general paused, regarding her for a moment. "You do not have enough natural Light for teleportation, Your Majesty," he said, and Hazel thought she caught a hint of mockery in his voice. "It is a high level technique, only possible for the most talented of Lightmakers."

She frowned. She'd only been joking, but it smarted all the same to know this was yet another thing Rydian had surpassed her in. When they'd first met, *he* had been the novice, while she had spent her whole life fighting.

"How is Johanas?" she asked, seeking to change the topic. "Has he woken yet?"

"Yes." Her heart turned over in her chest. "He and I have spoken. He refuses to help apprehend the outlaws."

Gods damnit Johanas!

"I'm sure I can convince him!" she said quickly.

"Very well."

Without further word, the general turned and started down the corridor in the direction of the meeting room. Hazel hurried after him, falling into step with the man as they turned a corner.

"Rydian can't have gone far, sir," she said, trying to

offer some reassurance. "We'll have the pair of Alfur back in custody in no time."

"Much as my personal matters still concern me, *Your Majesty*, I fear your friend's interference hints at a greater threat from this planet."

"Rydian is a fool, but he's not fool enough to threaten the Federation." She hesitated, unsure whether to mention what she'd seen in the meeting. It felt like a betrayal, even after Rydian had abandoned her, but if the general began to see Talamh itself as a threat. "Sir, I believe Rydian Holt's motivations are more...base in nature."

The general came to a stop. "Oh?"

She swallowed. "The Alfur, sir, Serena Levaanton. I believe the pair share a...fondness for one another."

"Such affairs are not unheard of," the general mused after a pause, his lips pursed in thought. "Though...you believe it is more than simple...pleasure?"

"I..." She bowed her head. "I believe so."

"I see." There was no mistaking the disgust in the man's voice now. He turned and started down the corridor, speaking as he walked. "If that is the case, then I cannot shield your friend from the weight of the Federation's judgement. To allow such an abomination would be to invite a parasite into the very soul of humanity. Rydian Holt and the Levaanton's must be hunted down and destroyed, before their corruption is allowed to spread."

Hazel's heart plummeted into her stomach. Her mouth hung open. She wanted to say she might be wrong, that she had only imagined the look the pair had shared, but...

...nothing else could explain Rydian's actions, surely? Not even Rydian Holt was such a fool to think he could go against the galaxy spanning Federation. He'd even said as much, before his treacherous little meeting had been interrupted.

"I...I understand, sir," she croaked.

"I'm glad to hear it." The general's eyes were cold as they stopped outside a door. Two guards stood to either side, ensuring no one came or went. They nodded as Colley reached for the door handle. "Now, let us see if this infamous Bloodlust can restore the honour to his name, or if he too chooses to side with the enemy."

He pushed open the door, then stood aside to allow Hazel to enter first.

"Well it's about time," a woman's voice greeted from within.

Hazel froze in the doorway. Reclining in a chair beside Johanas on the opposite side of the meeting table, Falcon waved back.

SEVENTEEN

Warmth wrapped Rydian in its fiery embrace. Light coalesced around him, banishing the darkness, filling him with wonder. It brought with it a sense of safety, that the monsters chasing him could not find him here. He lay in that brilliance for a long while, drifting, at peace...

He came awake with a start, heart racing, blind as he found himself in blackness. A simple thought solved that, as Light began to seep from his skin. Rydian breathed easier as the dark retreated.

He was still in the storage room. Serena lay alongside him, one warm arm draped across his chest, her eyes closed, breasts rising and falling gently as she slept.

Exhaling, Rydian settled back on the floor alongside her, though his heart did not slow. If anything, it quickened with the press of her body against him. They must have dozed off, afterwards. He swallowed, still not quite able to believe the fire he'd felt within, whether this was real, or...

...no, that was his own incessant insecurities rising. *This* Serena, the Serena that had kissed him with such fire, was not the trembling Alfurian captive he'd found in the arena. This was the Serena he'd once met blade to blade, the proud Alfurian princess who had fought for humanity against her own people's wishes. He didn't know when, or how, this bond had formed between them, but it didn't come from fear.

He too had felt that fear, knew that desperation to survive. This was not it.

Lying there on the cold floor with the warm Alfurian princess in his arms, those days felt like a long time ago, another life. He listened to the softness of her breath, felt the twin thudding of her hearts against his chest, and wondered how long this could last. If Colley had his way, they would both be dead within hours. But if his plan succeeded...

Rydian swallowed. Did he really have the courage to pull the trigger? He'd been willing to risk it all before, when he'd had nothing left to live for.

He'd allowed the darkness to return to the room, but a glint of Light came from elsewhere now, a faint pulse. Frowning, he sat up and looked around for the source, before realising it came from Serena's Manus reader. As he watched, it pulsed again. He was about to wake her when she jerked suddenly awake.

"What..." she mumbled, golden eyes blinking away

sleep. She held up her hand and frowned as the device pulsed yet again. "Is that..."

She squeezed her fist and a brilliant flash burst from the device. Light flooded into the air, swirling and churning until it finally took shape, becoming that of an Alfurian man. The Light offered no colour or fine details, but Rydian could see by the surprised look on the man's face that he was also seeing a projection of them—or perhaps just Serena.

"Serena Levaanton, is that really you?" A slightly distorted voice spoke.

"Willis?" Shock distorted Serena's voice as she gaped at the projection. "Willis Gardiner?

"It *is* you! A miracle! How are you still alive?"

"How am I still alive...Willis, how are *you* still alive? How do you have a Manus reader?"

The image flickered, as though the transmission was weak. Rydian could only stare. He'd used this ability once with Serena, connecting with her Manus reader through the Light. But the Alfur could only do it with their devices. Which meant this Willis still had his. The Federation had destroyed every device they could find. Did this mean some of Serena's people had escaped the conquest?

"When the Haze collapsed, Konad sent out a warning. I don't know whether the other cities received it in time, or if they even believed him, but here in Boustor...I thought it prudent to listen to the old bastard."

"You escaped?" Serena breathed. "You're free?"

A crackling filled the room as the image flickered

again. Obviously the transmission was struggling. He recalled Serena saying something about distance restrictions. More Light had solved that before, so he reached out a hand and gripped her wrist, allowing his own power to mingle with hers. The device brightened as she drew it through the crystal at its core, and the image immediately cleared.

At which point the projection of the Alfur cried out in fear. "Serena, who is with you! Have you betrayed us?"

He gestured wildly with his hand, as though trying to break the connection. But whatever Serena was doing with the Light Rydian had fed her, it must have prevented him from disconnecting, for the image remained as clear as ever.

"Peace, Willis. Rydian Holt is on our side."

"Rydian Holt? As in the human who almost *killed* you back in your Rotin days?"

Some of the colour fled Serena's cheeks in what Rydian was coming to learn was the Alfurian version of a blush.

"That would be the one."

"I also inadvertently helped destroy the Haze," Rydian decided to chip in, "though given I was a slave fighting back against his oppressive masters, you might sympathise with that somewhat nowadays."

A long silence followed from the hologram.

"And now you expect us to trust you, human?"

Rydian shrugged. "I don't expect much of anything

from you. Wasn't it *your* side trying to connect with Serena just now?"

Another pause. "I've been broadcasting to the other royal Light-signatures every week," he said eventually. "Not even sure why at this point. To prove to myself I wasn't the only one left, maybe."

"I'm not sure about the others...," Serena whispered. "I think...my father and I are all that remain in Goma."

"Aiden still lives?" Willis exclaimed. "That is good news. Surely he has a way to fight these scum—ah, invaders."

"He does not. But Rydian does."

"The human?" The eyes of the projection seemed to weigh Rydian up, before coming to a decision. "Whatever it is, the Alfur of Boustor will stand with you."

"That's very generous of you, ah, Willis, was it? But I'm afraid your people in Boustor are too far away to help in this fight."

"I can't believe it's really you," Serena spoke before the Alfur could argue. "And there are others as well?"

Willis nodded. "We fled into the caverns beneath Boustor, ones that were never fully explored. We've been hiding here ever since."

"How many, Willis?"

"I think its best I don't say, Serena."

Serena nodded. "I understand."

A pause. "It's...bad out there, isn't it?" Willis said at last. "You're the first person we've been able to contact in months. Is there...is there anything left, Serena?"

"*You* are still here, Willis. You and your people. Until this moment, I thought I was fighting only for my father and I." She exhaled slowly, golden eyes fixed on the hologram. "But you've given me hope. That there are others out there, others we can yet save."

The hologram's face flickered. "I...hope so, Serena. There are children with us, and without Light, they're little more than ghosts. We all are. I do not know how much longer we can last."

"Just a little longer, Willis," Serena whispered. "Rydian has a plan."

She looked at him as though in question.

"I do," he said simply.

Willis's face was grim, but after a long pause he nodded. "Then we will do our best to hold on, Serena Levaanton of Goma."

With that the image flickered and died.

Silence fell in the storage room. Rydian watched Serena, her face lit by the glow from the Manus reader. Her eyes were distant, her lips pursed in worry.

"Who was he?" he asked at last.

"The Alfurian Prince of Boustor. But he was like me, a Heir, until his father died ten years ago. The only one of the Council to have been born on Talamh."

"Then he has no idea..."

"Only what Konad managed to tell him. He was the oldest of the Princes. Always hated humanity. Now I know why." She exhaled softly. "I can't believe they escaped. I thought..." She didn't need to finish for Rydian to understand.

She thought everyone else she'd ever known was dead.

"Your plan?" she asked after a moment. "You really think it'll work?"

Rydian swallowed. *It has too.* Outwardly, he only nodded.

"Good." Serena's face hardened as she stood and offered him her hand. "Then we'd better go find out how Father and Jasmine are going with the machines."

Accepting her hand, Rydian allowed her to pull him to his feet. "Oh joy," he said, then despite himself, allowed a grin to spread across his lips. "I wonder what they're going to say when they see us together?"

Serena's eyes widened and some of the colour left her face.

EIGHTEEN

"Falcon, what are you doing here?"

Hazel stood frozen in the doorway, staring at the pair seated at the table. What the hell was happening here? Falcon had vanished with Rydian, hadn't she?

"What, you thought you could get rid of me that easily?" The woman reclined in her chair, feet up on the table.

Her picture of innocence was in stark contrast to the room, which still displayed the damage left by Johanas's battle with her soldiers. The dead and wounded had been removed, but the gaping hole in the window remained. Outside the wind was beginning to buffet the building and she could see dark clouds on the horizon.

"How the hell did she get in here?" Colley growled.

He turned to glare at the guards outside, but their faces showed only confusion. Hazel wandered inside, still somewhat dazed by Falcon's reappearance. She jumped as the door slammed closed. Nostrils flaring, Colley strode across the room and pressed his fists firmly against the table.

"Where is Rydian Holt?"

Hands entwined behind her head, Falcon raised both eyebrows. "How in the heavens would I know?"

"You disappeared along with him and the other traitors."

"Geeze," Falcon muttered. "Can't a gal go looking for a drink without everyone assuming she's a traitor?"

"A...drink?" Colley appeared momentarily at a loss for words.

"Yes, booze, liquor, hell, I'd take a spot of *ale* at this stage." Removing her hands from her head, she leaned forward across the table. "Don't suppose *you* know where a gal can get some?"

Hazel actually groaned. "Gods damnit, Falcon..."

Johanas, who had sat through all of this in silence, actually chuckled. A growl escaped Hazel as she swung on him.

"What's so funny?" she demanded. The grin immediately slipped from the big man's face. She shook her head. "I don't understand, Johanas. Why did you do it? Why fight for them? You *hate* fighting."

Hazel moved around the table until she stood at his side. He looked up at her, his face beaten black and blue, nose twisted. She'd never seen him in such a state. In his arena matches, most of his opponents had died without even leaving a scratch. A trickle of blood ran from his cracked lips as he forced a sad smile.

"Because someone had to do it, Hazel," he said quietly. "Because you wouldn't."

She clenched her fists. "They don't deserve our help, Johanas."

"Maybe. Maybe not."

"Were they worth your life?"

"Only the gods below can know that."

"Oh gods, enough with the soppy stuff!" Falcon interrupted.

"Yes, quite," Colley rumbled. Taking a seat, he folded his hands before him, hard eyes taking them in. "You promised he would talk, Your Majesty." The iron gaze flickered to Johanas. "So talk."

"Oh, so *this* is the guy the Federation put in charge of conquering the known universe?" Falcon interrupted. She stared at Colley for several moments. "Yeah, I see it."

"I already told you, general, I don't know what Rydian's plans are," Johanas replied, ignoring Falcon's comment.

"We know he might not have told you much," Hazel interjected quickly, allowing some of her desperation to leach into her voice. Johanas...Johanas didn't understand the kind of fire he was playing with here. "But we also know he visited you and Jasmine last night. He must have told you *something*."

The big man said nothing, but as he met her eyes, the sad twist remained to his lips.

"Ha, imagine that, old Rydian, with a plan." Falcon was having far too much fun for someone that was supposedly sober. "The only plan that boy could ever piece together was how to make big thing go *boom!*" She slapped her hand down on the table to emphasise her point.

"Seriously, Falcon," Hazel said through clenched teeth. "Why the hell are you even here? What purpose do you serve beyond being a human trash can? Can't you see I'm trying to save our world from destruction?"

"Oh, we're saving the world now, are we?" The woman snorted. "Sorry, can't keep up with all your internalised guilt coping mechanisms anymore."

"I'm not kidding—"

"Aren't you though?"

Hazel flinched. It wasn't Falcon who'd spoken this time. It was Johanas. His head lifted, until his eyes met hers.

"All this time, I thought you'd come around. That you were just trying to make the best from a bad situation. But...but now Rydian's back. Now we might have hope for something *better*. Better than the Federation. Better than what we had before. And what do you do?" He shook his head. "You're standing against him, Hazel. Standing with the enemy."

"The *Alfur* are the enemy!"

"The Alfur are broken, Hazel." His gaze drifted to the general. "They might have been monsters once, as you claim, general, but no more. On this planet, they learned to adapt, to find a more humane path. It wasn't perfect. Not by a long shot. But maybe together, we can be better, like Rydian says."

Hazel could only stare at Johanas, lost for words, but a snort of laughter came from the big man's other side.

"Ah but I missed you, Bloodlust. You're *almost* as mad as Rydian."

"Ay, it is a shame. I'd hoped to find at least one decent Lightmaker on this planet."

Something in the general's words warned Hazel. Screamed for her to act.

She wasn't fast enough.

Light *exploded.* Crackling, sizzling, *burning,* it burst from the general's raised hand and leapt across the room. Johanas barely had time to look up as the power engulfed him in that terrible glow. For a second the Goman gladiator was silhouetted amidst the brilliance, a stain, resisting against the all-consuming energies.

Then he was gone. Gone without so much as a whimper or plea for mercy. Just...vanished.

Hazel stood, arm outstretched towards her friend, the warning on her lips unspoken. She stared at the empty space, at the place where her friend had been sitting just a second ago. Not even the chair, not even ashes remained.

She couldn't tear her eyes away. He...Johanas couldn't be gone. He would reappear any second now, return from whatever...whatever punishment the general had sent him too...

Silence. Nothing. The general's power had wiped him from existence.

"...Hazel...Hazel?"

Someone was shaking her, saying her name, but with

the ringing in her ears, she couldn't understand. What was happening?

Crack!

Something hard struck her across the face. Crying out, she swung around and found Falcon standing over her. Hazel blinked. When had she laid down on the floor? She stared at the woman, still trying to work out what had happened, why it was Falcon standing there, and not...

"Where is Johanas?" she whispered.

A strong hand clasped her by the jaw, forcing Hazel to look the woman in the eyes.

"Gone, lass." Falcon's words were harsh, unyielding. Hazel wanted to flee from them, to deny them—

Falcon shook her. Hard.

"Gone! You hear me?" she repeated, teeth bared. "He's *dead*. And unless you want to end up the same way, I suggest you *wake the heavens up!*"

Hazel swallowed. Then...then she looked in her friend's eyes, and nodded.

"Good." Falcon released her and straightened. "Your general friend left when you lost your marbles, but he'll be back. And he didn't seem like the sort to waste time chatting."

"He...he wants Rydian..." Hazel whispered.

"Yeah, and his two little Alfur friends."

"What...what are we going to do?"

Falcon frowned. "I thought that much was obvious."

"We need to find Rydian."

Her friend's frown deepened. She held up a bottle. The liquid inside was *green*.

"Actually, I was thinking of something a little more productive."

Hazel groaned.

NINETEEN

Serena's face was *cold* with embarrassment.

She and Rydian had returned to the control room to find her father still fiddling with the computer and Jasmine putting the finishing touches on whatever repairs she'd made to the controller for the Haze. Being no mechanical expert, she couldn't see much change in the machine herself. But Jasmine was the one who'd spent close to a year locked up with these machines and their engineers. If anyone could fix the damn thing, it was probably her.

Neither she nor Rydian said anything about their... encounter as they entered, but Serena couldn't help but feel there was a knowing glint in their parents' eyes...or maybe that was just her imagination. It wasn't like her father was particularly adept in reading human emotions, and Jasmine still seemed uncomfortable enough with her son that she probably hadn't noticed anything.

She met the woman's eyes, and Jasmine *goddamn smiled*. Serena quickly looked away, the temperature plummeting further in her cheeks as her hearts palpitated uncomfortably.

Rydian didn't seem to notice. Moving to her father, he tapped him on the shoulder, then drew him away into the far corner. The pair proceeded to stare at one another in a way that suggested they were communicating telepathically.

"So." Serena almost jumped out of her skin as Jasmine spoke from directly behind her. Damn that woman could move quietly when she wanted too. "My son seems...fond of you."

"Ah..." Suddenly the floor between Serena's feet seemed incredibly interesting. This was *not* a conversation she'd wanted to have.

"I'm glad." A hand settled on Serena's shoulder. Her head jerked back up. She was surprised to find a wry smile on the woman's lips. "You know, I haven't exactly been the best mother. So I'm glad he found someone."

"I..." Damn, it was like a gigantic lump of coal had lodged itself in her throat. "I'm...glad too," she managed. Better than standing there with her mouth hanging open, she supposed.

It seemed to be enough for the woman, for she gave a short nod and turned around. But while she'd been distracted, Rydian and Aiden had finished their conversation, and now Serena's father was on his hands and knees inside one of the mechanisms. At the sound of

Jasmine's footsteps, he withdrew and gave a little wave towards her.

"It's okay, Mrs. Holt. I can handle these last adjustments."

Jasmine paused, a frown creasing her forehead, but Aiden's head had already disappeared back into the machine. Serena looked from her father to Rydian. What had the pair talked about? Her stomach twisted. Something was going on here. It better not put her father at risk.

She swallowed. After Jasmine's comments, the last thing she wanted was to invite similar remarks from her father, but...

She wandered over to join him beside the machines—then almost laughed at the sight of him. On his back with his head literally inside the machine, he looked about as far from a Prince as she'd ever seen him. Was this how he'd been, back in the early days of Talamh, when *he* had been the Heir, her grandfather the Prince?

"Did you find what you were looking for, Father?" she asked.

A grunt came from inside the machine and a hand emerged. "Could you hand me that wrench beside you?" he asked without withdrawing himself. She obliged, placing the tool in his long Alfurian fingers, before he finally replied to her question. "I did."

She sighed, slumping into the controller chair. "I don't suppose you're going to tell me what that was?"

"Not if I can help it, Daughter."

"What about your little conversation with Rydian?"

The sounds of metallic clanging inside the machine stopped for a moment as her father slid out from inside and looked her in the eye.

"I do not know, Daughter. Is there a secret you'd like to share about the two of you?"

"Ah...no, no, you ah, you know what, I think I'll go talk to him." Damnit, she was never this flustered.

Her father only smiled. "I thought as much."

Muttering profanities as she walked away, Serena looked around for Rydian. Why couldn't everyone just keep their nosy noses to themselves? She wasn't even sure what they *were*. It had just been one moment of intimacy, after all.

Serena clenched her fists. Why did she suddenly feel so unsure of herself? What did she care what they all thought? She'd spent half her long life rebelling against her father—especially against the way he'd treated the humans of Talamh. This...thing with Rydian, wasn't that just a natural progression of her rebellion? Maybe that's all it was, another way to spite the man who'd attempted to control her entire life.

Except it wasn't, was it?

Her mouth was inexplicably parched as she drew to a stop before Rydian. A smile lit his face when he turned and saw her there. She'd be damned if her hearts didn't do a little dance at that look. Her hands shook as she looked him in those crystal blue eyes.

She knew what the problem was. The terror that

cramped in her abdomen, twisting and churning, screaming for her to run.

Rydian would do anything to protect his planet, to protect her and the people of Talamh. She could see it in his eyes.

Anything, including sacrificing himself to save them all.

"Will it work?" she asked, her voice barely rising above a whisper. She didn't need to say what she meant. Hell, she still didn't know the exact details of his plan.

Rydian's eyebrows knitted themselves together in a frown. For a moment she thought he wouldn't answer, that their situation was truly so precarious, that he could not even bring himself to say the words out loud—

"It'll work."

The words were short and concise, softly spoken, as though he had projected all his strength and confidence into their announcement. She could tell Rydian was doing his best to reassure her.

He failed.

"You're going to turn the Haze back on, aren't you?"

He pursed his lips and for a second it seemed he would say more, but in the end, all he offered was a nod.

"And if you succeed, what then?" she whispered. "What happens to you when you turn it on, Rydian? What happens to your people?"

"They die." Jasmine's voice was cold as she approached. She held up her hand, which still had her old

Manus reader embedded in her palm. "For their greed and cruelty, they all die."

"No," Rydian said curtly. His eyes did not flinch from his mother's gaze. "That is *not* the plan."

"Then what is?" Serena interrupted. "To destroy yourself?"

"I..."

He trailed off as Serena reached into the box they'd brought from the storage room and held up a Manus reader. One of the human ones, designed to suppress their Light. If they were turning the Haze back on, this was the only thing that would prevent it from driving Rydian insane. The last time he'd been exposed to that terrible force, he'd been at the precipice of madness. One last push was all it would take to send him over.

"You don't have to destroy yourself, Rydian." She met his eyes, and saw the determination there. "This can protect you."

His Adam's apple bobbed up and down. "It could..." His eyes slid closed. "But I can't risk it, Serena."

Her fist tightened around the metallic cylinder. "Rydian, if you turn the Haze on without one..."

"You will become a threat to us all, Mr. Holt." Her father finished for her. He gave Rydian a knowing look. Behind them, the panels of the computer had been replaced. The repair job was apparently finished. "The cumulative damage you have suffered is enough that the Haze will shred your mind the second it returns."

Rydian grimaced. "Thank you for your concern,

Aiden," he said, "but if I suppress my power, we'll be help-less if Colley finds us before we're ready."

Serena's heart sank. He was right. Colley was powerful—and far more experienced than Rydian. Even with access to his Light, he would be hard pressed to stop the general. He'd taken the man by surprise in the arena, but in a fair fight, the outcome could prove quite different. She'd learnt that in the arena. No matter a man's raw power, training and experience often counted more.

And without his Light, well, Rydian wouldn't stand a chance.

Though...perhaps there was another way.

"You might not be able to protect us if you're suppressed," she breathed. Stepping in close to Rydian, she met his gaze, and smiled. "Do you trust me, Rydian Holt?"

TWENTY

The world was spinning. *A lot.* And there was this terrible green haze across her vision. She thought...she thought they'd gotten rid of...that.

Hazel hiccupped.

"Another!"

Hazel could barely hold her glass steady while Falcon poured the amber liquid. It was a different flask from the one they'd started on. Their third? Or was it the fifth? Who cared? All Hazel could focus on at this point was the desperate need to keep one hand firmly grasping the table. Otherwise the entire world might just spin away.

"Gods damnit, Falcon."

Glasses clinked. Liquid burned. The world got just a little bit foggier. Still, she couldn't hear them. The screams. So long as she couldn't hear the screams, she was okay...

Gods this stuff was awful. It burned as much on the

sixth shot as the first. She hardly cared at this point. Maybe she deserved the pain. For betraying her friends. For betraying her world. Would it burn like this when the gods condemned her to a fiery inferno? It didn't matter. It couldn't hurt half as bad as the pain in her chest, as the yawning chasm she felt with Johanas's absence.

"It...wasn't meant...to be like this," she slurred, resting her head against the table. "Being queen...meant to save them...save them all."

"Ha!" Falcon threw back her head and laughed—and very nearly toppled from her chair. "You weren't a queen, woman. Gods below, a queen never spent so much time on her knees begging for scraps. Nah, you weren't anything but a trumped up peacock the Federation put in charge so the rest of us wouldn't kick up a fuss about our latest conquerors."

Hazel winced. Despite the drink, the woman's words cut to the bone. "Screw you, Falcon," she snapped, lurching upright and pointing her empty glass at the ex-champion's face. "If you thought...the whole thing...was a farce...what the heavens...were you doing there...standing next to me."

"Why do you think, little Hawk?"

"Cause you're a good for nothing drunk!"

Falcon said nothing and silence fell across the conference room. Silence except for the whistling of wind through the broken window. Hazel shivered. Darkness was falling outside. Rising, she stumbled to the gap and swayed there, looking down on the city. On her city.

Lights shone across the sprawling slums, the only true change she'd accomplished since her ascension. To give her people the power the Alfur had denied them for so long. But what had that really changed? The humans of Talamh still toiled day in and day out just to support themselves and put food on their tables. The Alfur had been replaced by the Federation, but what did the average human care who ruled them?

"Because you needed someone."

She flinched at Falcon's voice. Looking back from the edge, she saw that Falcon had risen from her seat and was watching her with a look of concern. A lump lodged in Hazel's throat. She looked back at the window, at the yawning chasm below, on the city filled with people. They didn't care that Johanas was gone. Caring, peaceful Johanas, who had given so much of himself for them.

They wouldn't care if she fell either, she knew.

"Don't, Hazel," Falcon whispered.

She closed her eyes as a hand settled on her shoulder. "Why not?"

"Because that's not what he would have wanted."

"How do you know what he would have wanted?" Hazel croaked. "He hated what I became. Maybe he would have thought it better that I fall, rather than continue with this farce."

"Then don't continue it."

She clenched her fists. "We cannot defeat the Federation. You know that."

How many times did she have to say it? She didn't like

them anymore than the others, but Hazel was a realist. She had done what she could to make use of the Federation, to find a way to improve life on Talamh for her fellow men and women. To make her home a better place. That was all she'd wanted. Maybe if the others had done the same, instead of raging against the inevitable.

"*We* can't, but Rydian sure seemed convinced he could."

A shiver ran down Hazel's spine. Standing in the fresh breeze had steadied her vision a little now, sharpened her mind. That, and the Light. It burned up the alcohol in her blood, protecting her from the worst of its effects. Exactly what she didn't want. A sigh whispered from her lips as she stepped back from the edge and looked at Falcon.

"Did you really stay all this time, just to keep me company?"

Falcon looked away, though not before Hazel caught the glint of tears in her eyes. "It's what Aureli would have done," she said. "He...he would have known what to do. I'm sorry you kids only had me. I wish..." Her eyes slid closed and a tremor shook the former champion. "I wish I could have been the woman he wanted me to be. I'm sorry I couldn't give you anything more than my drunken company."

Hazel swallowed. She'd never asked the woman why she'd stayed these last months, why the former champion hadn't turned her back like the others. All this time, Hazel had assumed it was for the cushy apartment and the drink. She couldn't have been more wrong.

"Thank you," she managed at last. "I know I've never said it, but I'm glad I had you at my side."

Falcon snorted. "For all the good it did."

"Don't sell yourself short," Hazel said with a wry smile. "Truth be told, I don't think the Federation were ever really interested in helping us. Too rebellious, this planet. Too familiar with the Alfur, conditioned into believing them to be important. They couldn't have dangerous thoughts like that spreading through the galaxy, could they? No wonder they treated us like dirt, keeping us isolated."

"You think?" Falcon was suddenly thoughtful. "Why *would* they keep us isolated, if what they really wanted was to show us humanity's superiority. They could have brought more Alfurian slaves here, used their resources to show our people just what the Federation was capable of."

"That's what I've been trying to tell them for the last six months."

"And by all logic, they should have listened," Falcon mused. "Instead, they've done all they could to keep their secrets from us. It's almost as if..." Her frown deepened. "As if they're *afraid* of us."

Hazel snorted. "And what exactly would they be afraid of? A tiny pocket of resistance? A few free Alfur they missed in their planetary conquest? It's not like our human population could threaten them. We've spent our entire existence under the Haze, our powers suppressed. What could Talamh possibly have to threa—"

She cut herself off abruptly and stared at Falcon. The

woman stared back, the beginnings of a frown on her forehead. As one, the pair turned to gaze out the window. Not at the city this time, but up at the sky. The sky that had been green until just a few short months ago...

"You don't think..." Hazel murmured, turning back to Falcon.

She was surprised to find the colour drained from the woman's face. "I think if anyone was crazy enough..."

"...it would be Rydian."

"Gods."

"The Haze, he's going to switch it back on," Hazel croaked. "And turn it against them."

Falcon stared back at her, understanding dawning in her eyes—along with something else. Fear. Pure, unadulterated terror. The Haze had almost destroyed her once, back when no one had understood it. If Rydian turned it back on...

"That's...that's..." she rasped.

"That's why they haven't found them," Hazel said, her eyes falling to the floor, mind drifting down to the basement far beneath this tower. "They're still here, in the control room."

"We have to—"

Boom!

Hazel cried out and stumbled against Falcon as the door to the corridor exploded inwards. Acrid smoke swept through the room, before clearing to reveal the hulking form of General Colley. Teeth bared in a triumphant grin, he stepped into the room, the two guards at his back.

"Thank you, ladies. I knew leaving you alive would prove useful eventually." A burning Light formed in his hand as he spoke. "Don't worry, I'll give your regards to your friends before I send them to join you."

Hazel screamed as he pointed. Light of her own coalesced in her hand, but she knew it would not be enough to block his attack. The air crackled as the general's power leapt from his outstretched fingers.

But before it could consume them, she heard a whisper from behind. "Gods below, this better work."

A hand settled on Hazel's shoulder.

And the entire world turned to Light.

TWENTY-ONE

Rydian Holt drew in a long breath.

It was time.

The machines were ready. Well, as ready as his mother and Aiden could make them. No one knew for sure if all the components that had once powered the Haze remained in place.

He swallowed, looking around the room where it had all come to an end six months before. They'd been together then, filled with hope. Now...he shivered as he thought about Johanas and Hazel. They should have been here for this. To help him make this choice.

Exhaling, he met Serena's gaze. The Alfurian princess gave a little smile, the slightest incline of her head. He started to reach out his right hand to take hers, before remembering it had returned to a stump of broken flesh. Strange, even without the hand of Light, he still felt he could move his fingers.

After his hesitation, Rydian reached out instead with his left, though he had to be careful when their hands met. His palm was a ball of agony where Aiden had cut into his flesh to implant the new Manus reader.

It felt...strange to be cut off from the Light again. He'd gotten used to its presence this past year, even when it had come with the pain—and the screaming. Warmth brushed against his leg and he looked down to find Fatimah watching him. He couldn't hear the big cat's voice now, but he read the concern in her eyes and smiled.

"It's okay, my friend. I'm not going anywhere." *Not this time,* he added silently.

His fingers tightened around Serena's palm, their Manus readers pressing together. His stomach twisted at the responsibility he had placed on her shoulders, but he had to admit, she was right. He might, on a good day with ideal conditions, be a match for Colley. But the second the Haze was brought back online, he would be incapacitated if he was still touching his Light.

He'd been hoping to resist a few moments, long enough to enact the second phase of his plan. Aiden Levaanton had been quick to put down that idea. The damage to his prefrontal cortex had already been done. Rydian wasn't sure what that meant exactly, but the Alfur assured him there would be no 'resisting' the Haze this time.

So reluctantly, Rydian had done as Serena had suggested, and imbued her with every drop of Light he could draw from within himself.

Time would soon reveal whether that had been a good idea.

Shaking himself, Rydian released Serena and nodded to Fatimah, before moving to where Aiden and his mother stood by the nest of machines. He studied the pair as he approached. His mother's face had returned to the same hard, unyielding figure he recalled from his childhood. But Rydian was no longer a child. He could see the doubt that lingered beneath the surface of her face. He wondered if it had been the same, when Jasmine had led the first resistance against the Alfur.

And if his mother's face was the same as it had been all those months ago...Aiden Levaanton could not have been more changed. The Alfur had yet to regain the weight lost during his time imprisoned, but in truth it was not his physical features that had changed. Gone was the imperious Alfurian prince that had once condemned Rydian himself to death. And in his place, Rydian saw...a father, one willing to do whatever it took to protect his child.

"Aiden," he said, drawing to a stop before the pair. "Are the defences still in place?"

The Alfurian prince inclined his head in way of answer.

"Good." He hesitated then as a thought occurred to him. "What you did, to push the Light back from this area, would it protect a Lightmaker from the Haze?" Damn, he should have thought of that sooner. If the Federation soldiers already had protection...

"No," Aiden said after a moment's hesitation. "It is a

good thought, but the Haze is corrosive to any projection of the Light outside a physical object. Any attempt to mute an area larger than a matchbox would be excessively costly—and greater still the longer it needed to be maintained."

Rydian let out a sigh of relief and nodded his thanks. Only Aiden knew the full extent of his plan.

As though sensing Rydian's doubts, the Alfur grasped him by the shoulder and drew him away from Jasmine. When next he spoke, Aiden's words barely rose above a whisper.

"This is not an easy path you have set for yourself, Rydian Holt. Are you sure it is the one you wish to walk?"

"Sure?" Rydian grimaced. "I am sure of nothing, Aiden."

The Alfur said nothing for a long moment. His golden eyes were distant, and following his gaze, Rydian saw Serena crouched beside Fatimah, stroking the feline's enormous head. His stomach did several summersaults as the Alfur spoke again.

"If you are not sure, then perhaps it is time to turn back from the brink."

A lump lodged in Rydian's throat. "Colley will kill you."

"I have lived a long life, even for an Alfur," came Aiden's eventual response. "My daughter has not."

Another pause, this time on Rydian's behalf. "Would it be a good life though?" he asked, his voice not rising about a whisper. "I could protect her, but she would always be a slave, an animal in the eyes of everyone around us. I...I want better for us. For Talamh."

The golden eyes returned to Rydian. "Then are you sure of your path, Rydian Holt?"

Rydian swallowed as he met the prince's fiery gaze. "I am."

"Good."

The pair shared a brief smile before turning back to Jasmine. She stood with her arms crossed, one eyebrow raised as she watched them.

"If you two are quite done, it's about time we got started."

Rydian's smile faded. He nodded. Fingers clenched around the hard cylinder of his Manus reader. Time to see if the plan he had been crafting the past six months could succeed where so many others had failed. He met his mother's gaze.

Nodding, Jasmine turned towards the nest of machines and began to tap at the board of keys sitting in front of them—

Boom!

Light exploded across the room, its fiery tendrils lashing out, slamming into the stone floor and tearing metallic panels from the walls. Rydian cried out and threw up his severed hand, thinking to draw Light from within to defend himself, but as his mind reached for the chasm where his power normally resided, he found only emptiness.

Then Serena was there. Moving with the fluid speed

of the Alfur, she leapt between Rydian and the explosion. Light hissed from her Manus reader as she discharged a dozen blasts before Rydian could so much as blink. Each struck a projectile, disintegrated them before they could cause injury or damage to the machines.

Silence fell for a moment.

Then another flash. A pair of bodies slammed into the ground at Rydian's feet.

Hazel and Falcon.

"What the—"

Crack!

The far wall shook and more panels were torn loose, only to be hurled across the room by invisible forces. This time Serena intercepted with short sword in hand. She had retrieved it from the storage room once they'd decided on this path of action. The blade shone as it struck each object and tore them to pieces.

"Rydian!" He jerked as Hazel stumbled to her feet. "Rydian." Her words were slurred. It was clear both women had been drinking. "Rydian, I'm so sorry...never... never should have...he killed Johanas, Rydian!"

It was as though she'd driven a stake through his chest. He stared at his former friend, trying to make sense of her words.

"Johanas?" he rasped, mouth suddenly dry. No, it couldn't be. He would have felt it, sensed it...

...except even before he'd supressed his Light with the Manus reader, they could sense nothing from beyond this room. Not with Aiden's protections in place.

Rydian's Manus reader flickered as he grasped at Hazel with his left hand. "You're...you're lying." His fingers tightened as he shook her. She didn't resist. *"You're lying!"*

Hazel struggled for words, but at her side, Falcon's face was pale, her eyes fixed on the glow of Rydian's device.

"What have you done?" she whispered.

"Hazel!" Rydian screamed. "Tell me the truth!"

"I'm so sorry," she rasped. All the strength seemed to go from the Talamh queen then, as she sank to the floor. Rydian released her instead of allowing her weight to drag him down, staring as she wrapped her arms around her knees and began to rock herself. "So...so sorry. He's... coming for us."

"Rydian!" Before he could even begin to address the pain of Hazel's revelation, Falcon had him by the shoulders and was shaking him. "Rydian, you need to stop—"

Boom!

This time, the door into the chamber and half the wall disintegrated before their eyes. Serena did her best to deflect the projectiles as the entire steel wall was torn apart rivet by rivet, but she couldn't protect them from the shock wave. Without Light for reinforcement, it struck Rydian like a hammer and hurled him from his feet.

He lay on the ground as General Colley strode through the ruin the blast had left of the other side of the room.

"Well, well, well, looks like we have an infestation," he

rumbled. His fists were clenched, the Light within glowing so bright his flesh shone red.

Rydian's heart fell into the pit of his stomach. He reached once more for his power, but again it slipped away. He was helpless. There was only one thing that could stop Colley. He turned to his mother, only to find her lying slumped unconscious near the machinery.

"*No!*"

He tried to rise, but agony came from his leg. It had twisted when he fell. Then Fatimah was there, the enormous cat looming over him, shielding him from the approaching general. Laughter rang through the chamber as Colley saw the creature. He didn't pause in his advance.

"No," Rydian whispered.

Pushing the cat behind him, he gritted his teeth against the pain and forced himself to his feet. His mind raced. The machinery was just behind him, but he didn't know how to work it. Only Aiden and Jasmine understood it. Dust swirled about the room, obscuring the others. He had to pray the elderly Alfur would come through.

"So this is where the magic happens," the general mused as he came to a stop in the broken entrance. Arms clasped behind his back, he made a show of looking around the room. "Incredible. A shame I have to interrupt the show. Can't have you launching such a weapon against your own people." He tisked. "Truly, never did I think to encounter such treachery from my own people."

"You know nothing, Colley," Rydian said through clenched teeth.

Where were the others? He couldn't stand against this man, not without his power. He strained to reach his Light, to push past the block of the Manus reader. But just as it had done so many times before his release, the device only flickered a little brighter, and the Light slipped through his fingers like water.

Now Colley's eyes narrowed. "You've stunted your-self," he said suddenly. There was genuine surprise in his voice. "You really fear this Haze so much? What a shame." Light shone upon the general's face as he ignited his power. "I really was looking forward to our rematch."

"Maybe I can help with that, Colley." Serena's voice rang out as she stepped from the swirling dust, placing herself between Rydian and the general. "Or are you afraid to cross blades with an Alfur who hasn't been half-starved?"

As she spoke, Light burst from her skin, setting her aglow.

The general raised an eyebrow. "So you imbued the Alfurian girl with your power." He chuckled. "Naïve, but innovative. Still, you cannot truly think to stop me?"

Serena lifted her blade and pointed it at the general's chest. "Let's see, shall we?"

TWENTY-TWO

Serena Levaanton's hearts raced as she faced the Federation general. Light *thrummed* in her veins, so much that she practically vibrated with the power. How had Rydian held all this within him without rattling his own skeleton to pieces? Anymore, and Serena felt that she must surely explode.

It was more than that though. It was as though a veil had been removed from her vision. She could *see* the world, see the vibrations of power throughout it, how it swirled around the humans—and the great cat as well— filling them with an incredible glow. The ripples shifted and changed with each movement. No, *before* movement even, almost as though...

Serena saw the general's first move before he even made it.

Her hand snapped up as the man's power coalesced, her Manus reader blooming with Light. The twin forces leapt to meet one another, crackling forces that slammed together with a terrible *boom*. If not for the tight control of each combatant, the fight might have ended there, the entire room and subbasement and tower brought down upon their heads by the force of the explosion.

Instead, Serena caught the excess energies as they rebounded and drew them back through her Manus reader —even as she sensed the general doing the same. He wanted his vengeance, to destroy her father and put an end to Rydian's plans, but not to the point of self-destruction. That was something, she supposed.

A smile touched Serena's lips as she again raised the sword and fell into a fighting stance. "How about we decide this the old fashioned way, general."

The man's face twisted into a scowl. He remained untouched by the explosion, but in her heightened state, Serena didn't miss the tightening around his eyes. Doubt. This was a man used to seeing the Alfur cowed and broken. They certainly didn't manipulate Light in a manner capable of matching a warrior of his experience.

Her grin grew as she gestured him forward. "Unless you're afraid?"

A rumble sounded from deep in the general's chest. Light crackled, and twin blades of power burst into existence. Serena had already reinforced her blade, and exhaling, she readied herself for their next exchange.

The general moved in a burst of speed, so quick that to the unimbued in the room he would have appeared as barely a blur. Even with all the Light contained within,

Serena would have struggled to match the sheer acceleration.

Thankfully, she didn't need to match it. Again, the ripples warned her of his approach.

A metallic blade rose to meet the twin blades of Light.

Shrieks filled the room as the sword met forces it had never been forged to withstand—and held.

Snarling, Serena took the fight to the general.

Light filled her muscles with power as she struck, whipping her blade to the side and dragging the general's weapons with it, then lancing forward to stab at him. Colley lurched backwards, narrowly avoiding the piercing stab, then swung again with his own Light forged weapons.

Desperation. That was what the Light screamed now. The wild look in his eyes. Back in the arena, he had been calm and in control, toying with her before battering her aside.

But back then she'd had no Light left with which to fight.

Back then, she'd been starved, exhausted, despairing.

Not this time.

Light *blazed* from Serena as she batted aside his blades and attacked again. This time, even with all her foe's speed, the razor edge found its mark.

Colley grunted as he staggered back, blood seeping from the cut she'd opened across his chest. His eyes were wide and for a moment she saw the fear there, felt the sudden *terror*. This...he recognised this, remembered it from so long ago...

His face closed over. Teeth bared, his left hand blade shifted, reforming into a shield, while the right elongated, granting him greater reach. This time when he started towards her, it was not with the rushed, dismissive nature of moments before. He came at her as an equal.

"You are an impressive specimen, I'll admit," he grunted, "with a little time, you could have made an adequate plaything." Then he laughed. "But I think I'd rather cut that pretty head from your shoulders while your father watches."

Serena's teeth ground together at his words. She answered them with steel. Let him change strategies all he liked—today the general had finally met his match—

She threw herself flat against the ground, warned at the last moment by a sudden shift in the vibrations. She was barely in time, as the general's shield suddenly became a burst of power. It tore through the space she had occupied just a second before, disintegrating all in its path. If she had still been standing there...

...the general didn't allow her time to linger on the thought. Serena barely regained her feet in time to counter a blow from his longsword. Sparks flashed as their blades came together—and now it was Serena's turn to curse as the fiery tip tore across her bicep. She leapt back as the general followed the blow with a lazy swing of his sword. His smile had returned.

"Impressive, but alas, an Alfur still," he continued his

line of thought. "The fool might have granted you power, but it is finite. You will fail, like all your people fail. Eventually."

He was right. She had barely sensed that last Light blast in time. The vibrations—or her sense of them—were fading, reducing her ability to predict his movements. She was burning through the Light Rydian had given her at a prodigious rate, just to keep herself in the fight. A few more minutes of this, and she would be just as helpless as their first encounter back in the arena.

A glance around the room showed the state of her companions. They were scattered and in disarray. Jasmine was on the ground, her father at her side. Rydian was moving towards them, but neither looked in any state to operate the computers that would activate the Haze. Without it...

Swallowing, she looked back at the general, her fist tightening around the short sword.

Her time might be limited, but she had not spent it all yet.

Serena would make it count.

TWENTY-THREE

Hazel couldn't understand how it had all gone so wrong. Johanas was dead. Rydian hated her. Now the whole planet might be destroyed by an enraged Federation general. For all she knew, he could do it himself, after the clash she'd just witnessed between the man and the Alfurian princess.

But...what did she care? She had done her best, and failed. Not just failed—she had been condemned by everyone she'd ever known just for trying.

So instead, Hazel closed her eyes and embraced the spinning in her head, the hazy call of the alcohol—

"Oh gods...snap out of it...please would you!"

Slap!

An open hand struck Hazel across the face before she could process the words. Reeling, she slumped against the ground and found herself staring at Falcon. The woman... the woman had seen better days. Her eyes were wide and wild, her lips parted as she panted, fists clenched as though she were about to scream.

"Hazel, gods, come on, I need you, the Haze!"

Hazel blinked. The woman's sheer desperation cut through some of her own panic. A hand was extended to her, and without thinking she took it. The powerful ex-gladiator dragged her to her feet—and into an embrace.

"They're going to turn it back on." Suddenly, Falcon was sobbing into her shoulder. "Gods, I can't...I can't do it again."

Awkwardly, she tried to hug the woman back. "It's okay, we can stop—"

"No." Falcon pulled away abruptly. For a moment, her eyes were clear. "No, we have to *help* them."

Hazel stared at her friend. "But that means..."

"I know."

"You might—"

"*I know.*" A tremor passed through Falcon's face. "It doesn't matter." She looked at the bank of computers. "Hazel, you have to help them."

She opened her mouth to argue further, but a cry from Serena drew their attention back to the battle between man and Alfur. A stone settled in Hazel's stomach. After initially being on the backfoot, the general seemed to have gained the initiative. She looked at Falcon.

"What about you?"

Light crackled as the former Goman champion stepped back from her, a blade of pure energy forming in her hands.

"About time I found out how well these off-worlders fight."

Then she was gone, darting across the room to join the battle. Light blazed from her flesh as she added her blade to that of Serena's. Hazel swallowed as she watched the two launch an attack against the general. Buying them time.

Buying *her* time.

With an effort of will, she tore her gaze away. The weight of responsibility settled on her shoulders as she started towards the bank of computers. Last time she'd been here, it had been Hazel who had destroyed them, who had brought down the Haze and invited the Federation to their planet.

Now she would do her best to right that mistake.

For Johanas. For Falcon. For Talamh.

She heard Jasmine's voice as she neared. The woman was awake, but she hadn't moved from the ground. Rydian and the Alfurian Prince crouched over her, talking quickly. They looked around at her approach, faces filled with fear and concern.

"Hazel," Rydian said, his voice cold as he rose.

"What's wrong with her?" she asked, ignoring the accusation in his tone.

Rydian's face flickered, his eyes darting back to the prone form of Jasmine. "Something struck her from the blast. She can't move." His face twisted in pain, before he quickly recomposed himself. "We're...trying to get the instructions for the machines from her, but...they're complicated."

"I can do it."

Rydian's eyes widened, but after only a second's hesitation, he shook his head. "I'm sorry, but we can't trust you, Hazel."

Hazel couldn't blame him. She really couldn't, after all this time, and everything that had come between them. But in that moment, she didn't care. Falcon had begged her to do this. And Johanas was *dead*.

She was done playing nice.

Choosing to ignore what Rydian had said, she pushed past him and sank into the chair in front of the bank of computers. After learning these machines had been responsible for oppressing her people for so many decades, she had made it a priority to study their use in the months since the conquest—both those few the Federation had acquiesced to sending here, and some from the Alfur that hadn't been destroyed.

At the press of a button, the bank of screens flickered to life. "Jasmine," she said briskly, "I'm ready. Tell me what to do."

Rydian stood between them, frozen with one hand extended towards her. He made no move against her though. With his powers locked behind the Manus reader, there was little he could have done anyway.

After a long moment, the whisper of a voice came from the floor—Jasmine. "Why are you doing this?"

Hazel grimaced, not taking her eyes from the screens.

"How about we debate my motivations for saving the world when there isn't a Federation general breathing down our necks?"

Another explosion rocked the room. The combatants must have been doing something to contain the blasts, for no shockwave reached their group. But a glance over her shoulder confirmed Hazel's worst suspicions. Even with Falcon's help, Serena was fighting a losing battle.

"Jasmine," she said again. "Now or never."

"Fine."

There was no love lost in the woman's voice, but she didn't hesitate any further. Hazel's fingers flew over the keys as the woman began firing off instructions.

"How long will this take?" Rydian asked, hanging over her shoulder.

"Five minutes," Jasmine paused her instructions long enough to answer her son. "Longer if you all keep talking."

"Do we have that long?"

Hazel swallowed, her fingers picking up the pace.

Another set of footsteps approached. Aiden Levaanton. "If not...I will buy us the time we need."

TWENTY-FOUR

Fire burned in Serena's veins. Together with the human, Falcon, she faced the Federation general—and fought him to a standstill. Her Light was fading fast now, slipping through her fingers, so that her every movement was slower than her last.

Falcon wasn't much better.

And yet still they fought. Serena no longer even knew why. She had given up on a victory long ago. She'd been a fool to even think it. Even with all her skill, with the natural agility of her Alfurian body, even with Rydian's Light, the general had her beat. For what was her skill, besides the centuries of practice this man had enjoyed?

You fight for your people! she shouted the words in the quiet of her mind. *For your father, for Talamh!*

Yet as the minutes ticked past and her energies dwindled, she found the words rung hollow. Afterall, had she not betrayed her people, tricked her father? How could one capable of such treachery deserve freedom?

A blow from Falcon sent the general back a step, his feet moving quickly to maintain his balance. Serena charged in anyway, blade held close. Their swords met, Light to steel, crackling in the quiet of the buried chamber.

Then the second blade reformed in the general's free hand. Serena's eyes widened as he raised it high, and tried to twist away, but found her own blade entangled. To her relief though, Falcon charged in and blocked the next blow.

Together, each blade locked to one of Colley's, they *pushed*.

And the general actually *budged*.

He staggered backwards one step, then another, before the metal walls brought him up short. Light thrummed from the general's skin as he bared his teeth, determination revealed in every inch of his face. The wall groaned, its panels buckling beneath the force of Light-infused bodies—

Abruptly, the general crumpled. His blades vanished, allowing Serena's and Falcon's weapons to plunge forward into the space he had occupied and onwards into the wall. Steel shrieked as they sliced deep.

Serena reacted first. Tearing her sword loose, she screamed with unexpected triumph, and brought it down—

The general vanished.

Vibrations.

Serena spun, diverting her sword to raise it high, as twin blades of Light descended. Sparks clashed and she gasped as the force drove her backwards, slamming her into the wall. Teeth bared, she looked up into the smug face of Colley. The familiar smile still twisted his lips.

"Almost," he whispered.

Then Falcon was there, and the chamber rung once more with the clash of blades and grunt of spent breaths.

Serena was left behind, panting against the wall, still struggling to understand how the general had so nearly gotten the drop on her. It was a moment before she noticed the change.

Silence.

The vibrations were gone. She could no longer feel them.

Fear touched her then. Light burned within, but it was no longer enough for Serena to predict the general's movements. If she returned to the fight...

A tremor shook her. She tightened her grip around the hilt of her sword, watching as the pair leapt back from one another. Falcon was panting, the Light beneath her skin stuttering, as though about to run out. The woman couldn't hold on much longer, especially not alone.

Then Serena finally noticed the movement at the back of the room. Her father, bent over a computer. Hazel at another, while Rydian crouched beside his mother, lips moving as he shouted some instruction.

They were still trying to turn the Haze on.

All was not lost.

The trembling in her hands ceased. With a snarl, Serena hurled herself at Colley's back.

For a moment, it seemed he had forgotten her, that she might strike a miraculous blow and drive her sword through his spine. Only at the last minute did he flicker. A voice screamed a warning—Falcon—but it was already too late. Serena's sword was already descending, plunging for the base of the general's skull.

It all happened in a moment. A blast of Light shot from the general, catching Falcon full in the chest and hurling her across the room. Then he was spinning, faster than her eyes could track, and now it was no longer the general's back that faced Serena, but his glimmering eyes.

His lips split in a triumphant grin. Fire tore through Serena's abdomen as his blade found its mark, even as his second deflected her blow.

A gasp slipped from her lips as she slumped against the man, her strength washed away like driftwood upon the tide.

"I told you it would not last," he rasped, his lips to her ear.

Serena jerked as the Light imbued in the general's weapon detonated, sending searing power into her already strained Light channels. Stiffening, she tried to open her mouth to scream, but found her voice had fled. A terrible, rasping whispered from her throat instead as she jerked and twisted, suffering in silent agony.

A heavy hand settled on her shoulder, pushing her down. She tried to resist, but Serena's strength had fled with the Light. Slumping to her knees, she looked up into the eyes of her killer.

Still grinning, Colley raised a fresh blade, poised to strike. There was no sign of Falcon. No one who could save her now.

"Any last words, Alfur?"

Serena's blade lay at her feet. She'd dropped it when Colley had deflected her strike. So close. If only she had the strength, maybe she could...but her hands, just like the rest of her body, refused to obey. Even the pounding in her chest was muted, her secondary heart barely stirring from the damage Colley's attack had done.

The general was watching her still, waiting for some acknowledgement. She would not give it to him. Her gaze slipped by him, seeking Rydian. Had she bought him the time he needed? If this was all for naught...

...Serena's eyes found her father instead.

"Colley. Stop."

The general froze at her father's voice. He remained staring down at her a few seconds longer. Then with a long exhale, he turned his back.

That hurt. Serena raged at the dismissal, that he thought so little of her...but he was right. She had nothing left to give. And a part, a part of her was relieved. Relieved her father had brought her a few moments more of life.

"What is it, Levaanton?" Colley asked. "Don't tell me you've come to beg for your daughter's life? That offer expired as soon as you all started talking about revolution.

The humans of this planet will be lucky if I don't send them back to the stone ages."

A sad smile touched Aiden's lips. "I thought you might want to see your daughter one last time, Colley."

Watching the general, Serena caught the flickering of emotion that passed across his face. Shock, fear, *anger*.

"What game are you playing, Levaanton?"

"No games, Colley," Aiden murmured. "No tricks." Turning to the bank of computers, he reached out and pressed a button.

One of the monitors flickered as the dark glass was lit from behind. All eyes in the chamber turned to stare as something took shape. A grainy, slightly blurred image appeared, showing a human woman lying in bed, swathed in a white medical gown. An Alfur stood beside the bed. It took a moment for Serena to recognise her father, young as he was in the video.

A gasp came from the woman in the bed, followed by a high-pitched cry. Her father reached out both hands and clasped them around the woman. At his touch, her screams faded and she slumped back against the pillows, panting softly.

The respite only lasted a few moments before the woman shrieked again. She was giving birth.

"What...what is this?" Colley whispered. "My Clari-bel...why, why are you showing me this?"

Serena couldn't tear her eyes from the screen. That woman...she looked so familiar, and yet so foreign. Serena knew in her heart she'd never met the woman before, and yet...

Her father sat on the side of the bed, holding the woman's hand. As the contractions continued, he stroked her hair. His whispered voice could be heard over the speakers as he reassured her. As she...as she gave birth to...

"This was why we had to hide, Colley," her father whispered. "Why she and I plotted together to create the Haze. To keep the Federation from discovering what we had done."

Serena's hearts were racing so fast she thought they might burst. Not even the agony in her stomach was enough to distract her from the woman on the screen. Thankfully, her control over the Light was slowly returning, her Alfurian biology directing it towards the wound, accelerating her own healing processes.

"No, it's not possible. A thousand years, and never..." Colley was mumbling.

"Never, until my daughter. Until your granddaughter."

"Father."

Aiden's eyes met hers from across the room. "I am sorry I never told you, Daughter."

Her hearts fluttered. More lies. Yet with this final truth, something about the world finally clicked into place. Why she had never quite felt right amongst the Alfur. Why she had been so drawn to humanity, to their traditions and behaviours. Why her blood raced at the thought of combat. And of Rydian.

"She..." Colley's head snapped around, eyes wide. "She can't be..."

"She is." Aiden's voice was soft. "I kept this video all these years, as a memory. Claribel did not survive her birth. It was the day of my greatest triumph, and greatest grief. The fate of our world was forever changed that day. Even now, I wonder if we might have fixed the Haze, if she had still been here, if we'd still had her brilliance."

Serena drew in a long breath, unsure now what to do. She allowed the Light to continue trickling into her wound, and her vision recovered a little more.

"No, no, no," Colley's eyes were wild, his words stumbling over themselves. "She was...you took her...can't be!"

He swung from Serena to her father, but not before she glimpsed the moment his confusion shifted to madness. All the sorrow and grief drained from his face, leaving only...only a terrible intensity.

A horrible realisation came to her then. That it didn't matter to this man who she was, what had passed. And she saw...saw the horrible conviction in his eyes. The decision he had come too.

"I don't know what you thought to gain from this, Levaanton," he breathed. "Showing me these lies, did you...did you truly think they would turn aside my blade."

"There is no lie, Colley. She is your granddaughter."

The general's lips thinned. "I think not."

Light flashed as the blades reappeared in his hands.

But as he raised them high, movement came from the

rear of the room. Hazel. The queen of Goma wore a grim smile as she rose from her chair.

"There," she proclaimed. Her eyes met Colley's from across the room. "It's done."

"What's done?"

The wrinkles at the edges of Hazel's eyes twitched. "Let's find out, shall we?"

With that, she reached down and pressed a button.

TWENTY-FIVE

Even shielded by his Manus reader, Rydian felt the change when Hazel pressed the button.

Felt the Haze return to Talamh.

The screams were instant, as a thousand, thousand fiery hooks lashed the minds of every Light imbued creature on the planet. Connected in an instant, they suffered as one.

Worse still though were the screams from inside the room in which he stood. The cries of his friends.

Across the chamber, Falcon had just regained her feet, but now she crumpled, thrashing wildly on the floor as her fingers tore at her face. Behind him, Hazel slumped against the machinery, her face, pale, breath coming in raged gasps. A harsh howl filled the room as Fatimah cried out—then fled through the shattered wall, eyes maddened.

Of the humans present, only Rydian and his mother were unaffected. He cast her a quick glance and their eyes met. Her face was grey, her pale lips pursed. His heart twisted. She didn't look good. And despite everything that had passed between them...she was still his mother.

But there was no time to linger on her injuries.

He forced his gaze to the centre of the room, where General Colley had towered over them all. This was the riskiest piece of the plan. Colley was powerful, which meant the Haze would be all the more painful for him. But this was also the first time he'd been exposed to the noxious force. According to Falcon, back when she and the other Goman gladiators had secretly disabled their Manus readers, it had taken weeks, if not months, for them to succumb to the maddening nature of the Haze.

Rydian was gambling the general's raw power was enough for the Haze to incapacitate him.

It looked like his gamble had paid off.

A groan of sheer agony slipped from the man's lips. The shimmering blades of Light vanished from his hands, leaving him standing there, swaying slightly on his feet, as though a light breeze might blow him over. His face had lost all its colour, turning to a pallid, sickly grey. He tried to take one trembling step, but his legs buckled and he sank to one knee, his breath coming in ragged gasps.

Rydian watched, dispassionate, as the general suffered. He cared nothing for this man. Not after what he'd done to Serena. To Johanas. He clenched his fists, trembling with anger. If it were up to him, he would leave the man like this, to suffer the agony his victims across the universe had suffered.

But this was not about Rydian. This wasn't about revenge, not this time.

This time, Rydian was fighting for all the peoples of Talamh.

So stepping over to the machine Hazel was slumped at, Rydian stretched out a finger and pressed the button she had used to reactivate the Haze. There was a faint *popping* sound in Rydian's mind, and then silence returned.

Hazel was the first to recover. With a groan and shake of her head, she straightened in her chair. Blinking, she looked around, a look of confusion on her face. It turned to surprise when she found Rydian standing over her.

"Rydian, wha...what happened? Why did it stop?"

"Aiden, help her make the last adjustments. Quickly."

There was no time for belated explanations. He turned and walked towards the general, sweeping up Serena's discarded sword as he went. Colley was still on the ground, hands clasped over his ears, but as Rydian approached, the man jerked and seemed to remember himself. Lines creased his forehead as he looked up—then seeing Rydian standing over him—swept to his feet in one fluid movement.

"So that was your secret weapon," he said, doing a pretty good job of acting like he hadn't just been on his knees. "Impressive, I'll admit. But you will need more than the likes of that to defeat the Federation, Rydian Holt."

"Unpleasant, is it not?" Rydian murmured. His gaze travelled past the man, to where Serena was on the ground. She didn't look to be in a good way either. His fist tightened around the hilt of Serena's blade, but he made no move against the man. Not yet.

"A device created by the Alfur to destroy us," the general agreed. "A device they used to suppress your own people. It makes one question how it is you still fight for them. Surely such a crime screams out for vengeance?"

Rydian shrugged. He could feel the Manus reader pressing against the sword hilt. Drawing in a breath against the pain, he squeezed harder, until he felt something go *crack*.

It was like darkness had turned once more to day. Light flooded him as the device failed, burning away the pain of his wound, coalescing from his broken stump to form his lost hand anew. From one moment to the next, he went from bowed and broken, to warrior ready for battle.

The sight brought a smile to Colley's face. "Ah, so you have decided at last to test yourself against me."

"No," Rydian murmured. "No, I do not intend to fight."

So saying, he turned his back on the general and walked to where Serena lay. This was a terrible gamble, he knew, but Aiden and Hazel needed time to make the final adjustments. The general had a taste of the Haze, understood the corrosive force it represented. Now...

...now they would turn it against far more than just one Federation general.

Serena's golden eyes opened as he approached, a grimace touching her lips. "Wasn't quite...fast enough."

Her hands were wrapped around her belly, where Colley's blade had pierced her. It would have been a fatal blow for any human, but he prayed her Alfurian biology and a spot of Light would save her from the worst.

"You did more than enough," he said with a smile. "Here, take some of my Light."

He laid a hand on her shoulder, but she stopped him before he could imbue her with his power.

"No," she rasped. "Have...enough to heal. He... damaged my Light channels. Any more...would only hurt..." A twist came to her lips. "Besides, you might need it yourself."

A lump lodged in Rydian's throat at her words. He hesitated, but finally nodded. "You rest here then," he said and straightened. Turning, he found himself face to face with Colley.

"Do you make a habit of turning your back on enemies?"

"I see you didn't take the opening."

"No." The general's lips thinned. "Just as you did not strike me while I was incapacitated. Why? Some naïve belief in rehabilitation, maybe?"

Rydian chuckled. "There was once a child who would have thought so." He narrowed his eyes. "The Alfur killed that child. The man who remains isn't so foolish as to think you'll change, Colley."

"Then why?"

From where Rydian now stood, he could see Hazel and Aiden at the machine. In that moment, the Alfurian prince looked up. Golden eyes met Rydian's. And the man nodded.

Looking back to the general, Rydian allowed himself a smile.

"Because I needed you alive, Colley."

It was somewhat satisfying to watch the smug look slip from the general's face. Though to the man's credit, he managed to keep his cool.

"Oh?"

Rydian took a step closer, until barely an inch separated them. Light burned within each, their power filling the room.

"I need you to deliver a message to the Federation."

The general's lips thinned, but he raised an eyebrow. "And what message is that, Mr. Holt?"

Teeth clenched, Rydian refused to back down, to allow his face to betray even a hint of weakness. Everything he'd been working towards, everything he'd planned had been leading up to this moment.

"Talamh is off-limits," he breathed.

"Is that so?" A smile cracked the general's face. "Off-limits ay? I think we could manage that." Laughter, cruel and dark, rumbled from the man's chest. "Yes, I don't think any of our people will need to step foot on this God forsaken planet before we blast its surface clean from space." He paused, and his eyes hardened like crystal. "Would that suffice for a message, Mr Holt?"

Rydian chuckled. "You really are something else, Colley."

He started forward, sword still in hand. The general tensed, but Rydian made no move to attack, and walked straight past the general to approach the others once more. Colley watched him go, eyes narrowed.

"Is it done?" Rydian asked Aiden.

The Alfur offered a solemn nod.

"Good." Rydian turned to regard the general. "I never told you, Colley, but during my time with your people, your *Federation*, I came to a grim conclusion about humanity. About humanity and the Alfur both." Crossing his arms, he cast his eyes around the room, taking in Falcon, and Serena, and Hazel and Jasmine and Aiden. And Colley. "None of us are worthy of the blessing we were given. The Light that burns within all of us should have been a great gift, a path towards peace and paradise." He shook his head. "But what did we use it for instead? War. First the Alfur, then humanity. Then both."

His eyes fell to the Manus reader in his own palm. The crystal had cracked, allowing his powers to return.

"So I came to a decision, while I was recovering." He looked up and met the general's gaze. "That I would return to Talamh, and find a way to destroy the Light."

"Impossible. The Light is the core of everything. Without it—"

"The universe would cease to function. So I understand." Rydian smiled. "So instead, I thought to find a way to deny us its power. To amplify the signal generated by the Haze, and broadcast it across the galaxy. So anyone that touches the Light will suffer as you just suffered now."

Silence.

"Holy s—" Falcon muttered, sitting up from the floor.

"Rydian..." Serena's voice was soft, but stronger than before.

The others remained silent. They had already seen what Aiden and Hazel had been doing.

Rydian reached out a finger so that it hovered over the button that would turn the Haze back on. Turn it back on, and broadcast it across the stars. His insides twisted in terror at what that would mean, the countless lives he would destroy, all of them, wiped out in the cruellest of ways.

The general was watching him, eyes hard, arms crossed. "You wouldn't."

Rydian swallowed. "You're right," he said, then grinned. "I would prefer not to resort to such an extreme measure." He hardened his face again. "But I will do what is necessary to protect my people, even if it means destroying us all."

For a long moment, Colley said nothing, only stared at Rydian and his friends, stared until Rydian was sure he would call the bluff...

"Your message," the general murmured.

It took all Rydian's will not to let out a sigh of relief. He inclined his head instead. "My message," he agreed. "And one addition. Over the next few months, Talamh will begin sending out transport ships. Ships loaded with these." He held up his hand to demonstrate the bloody Manus reader. "They will be available for any who wish to protect themselves from the Haze. A second kind will be made for the Alfur, as a system to feed them the Light they require to live. Both will come at a cost—the Light itself. No more will our species battle one another with such power. We will live—and die—as mortals."

"Why would we agree to that? If we leave your planet alone, there is no reason to unleash this vile weapon."

"I already told you why," Rydian replied, steadfast in his conviction. "Our species do not deserve the Light. So I'm giving humanity and the Alfur one year. Then the Haze will destroy anyone who still clings to their power."

It would be a difficult year, he knew. The Federation would try and find a way to destroy them, of destroying the Haze before it could activate. They would need to use the equipment in this room—and in the other cities—to monitor for potential attacks. And someone would have to be ready at any moment to flip the switch.

But it would all be worth it, if they could rid themselves of men like Colley. Of men who thought they could rule the galaxy with this power.

"The Federation will never accept this."

"Then I suggest you make them, Colley," Rydian snapped. "Or the last thing you and everyone else will know is the madness of the Haze. You've felt it—is that how you wish for the great General Colley to end? As a whimpering wreck, huddled on the floor, begging for mercy as his mind wastes away to nothing?"

The general's eyes never left Rydian's. There was no missing the hatred there. This man would hunt Rydian until the ends of his days. That was fine. Let him stew in his anger. So long as his fear was stronger. So long as he was the first to flinch. That was why he'd needed to unleash it once, if only for a moment. To show the general what it was he faced, what it was he risked.

The Light within Colley surged. Rydian tensed as he sensed the gathering power, readying himself...but the general made no move to attack.

"I will deliver your message, Rydian Holt," he said instead.

Then the Federation general vanished in a flash of Light.

EPILOGUE

ONE YEAR LATER

Rydian stepped back as the last brick was set in place. The final stone that would complete the transformation, and convert the Goman arena from a place of death, to one of healing. In truth, that transformation had begun long ago, when Johanas and his mother had taken it upon themselves to treat the wounded gladiators.

But no longer would men and women from across Talamh journey to this place to fight and die for the entertainment of the bloodthirsty crowds. Now...now they would come to visit the human and Alfurian doctors of the Goman Memorial Hospital, come to be healed, to be saved.

Gods below, how Rydian wished Johanas and his mother could have been here to see it.

Not even Aiden Levaanton's healing Light had been enough to save Jasmine from her injuries on that dark day. Deep beneath the ground, in the aftermath of their victory over Colley, Rydian had said his goodbyes, and heard her regrets, listened to her words of love. Even a year later, the memory still brought tears to his eyes.

And Johanas. Poor, noble Johanas. He had deserved so much better than this world had given him. Rydian hoped wherever death had taken his friend, that debt would be repaid. It was the least the man deserved, after everything he'd sacrificed.

It still pained Rydian that he had failed to save his friend. His friend, and so many others. In the end, his decisions had protected Talamh from Federation control. But the universe...well, today they would find out whether the universe too could find the strength to fight back. To win their own freedom.

A smile touched his lips as he thought of the man who had brought him home. Captain Briggs. He'd seemed a good sort, willing to see the Alfur as more than the Federation had taught him. If the universe was filled with humans like Briggs, well, maybe they had a chance after all.

"Are you ready?"

He looked around at Serena's voice. His heart gave a little flutter when he saw her wandering through the crowd tow. A few gave little mutters at her passing, but most only nodded greetings at her passage.

A lot had changed in a year.

A lump lodged in Rydian's throat as Serena came to a stop before him, hands clutched over her swollen belly.

What changes would the next year bring?

"I'm ready," he said, and kissed her.

She kissed him back, arms wrapping around his waist as they enjoyed one last moment connected through the Light. Intertwined with the power of the universe.

Then letting out a long breath, they stepped apart and Rydian raised his hand. They had replaced the broken old Manus reader with a new version, one that was a combination of the old human models, and the Alfurian ones. It would filter enough Light through his system to maintain his artificial hand, and not much more than that. Maybe create a bit of illumination or allow communication over long distances.

All across Talamh, and the rest of the galaxy, millions upon millions now wore the same device, in preparation for this day.

His device was unique in one way only. It contained a switch, one that, once pushed, could never be turned back off again. A remote control for the Haze. Several moments over the last year, Rydian had feared it would need to be used early. Like when Federation ships had sailed close to Talamh, only backing down once contact had been made reminding them of the treaty, and the consequences of breaking it.

But now...now the time had come.

No more hesitation.

Reaching down, Rydian pressed his thumb to the control switch on the device.

A great whirring could be momentarily heard from the towers overhead, as mechanisms that had slept for a year returned to movement. Whirring turned to a faint buzzing, before overhead the sapphire skies began to change. Emerald bled across the great expanse, as the heavens of Talamh succumbed to the twisted nature of the Haze.

And silence fell across the universe.

NEXT up why not check out something different with my very first novel, Stormwielder, and don't forget to leave a review.

NOTE FROM THE AUTHOR

Huh, well, I'm not quite sure what the moral lesson of that story was. The characters kinda directed me there. Imagining how each of them would react to the discovery of a human federation beyond Talamh, and the crimes of their own species, was an interesting phycological exercise. But getting into my characters heads is always my favorite part of writing.

Anyway, if you've made it this far, I hope you've enjoyed the series. It was a bit of a diversion from my usual epic fantasy stuff, being shorter and more science fiction in nature. I'm enjoying the change of pace of these different story, but my next series I do believe will be a return to form as I explore an all new epic fantasy world. If that sounds interesting to you, make sure you give me a follow below so you can keep up with my work!

FOLLOW AARON HODGES

Join Aaron Hodges on his newsletter to **receive TWO FREE novels and a short story!**

https://aaronhodgesauthor.com/newsletter

ALSO BY AARON HODGES

The Sword of Light

Book 1: Stormwielder

Book 2: Firestorm

Book 3: Soul Blade

The Legend of the Gods

Book 1: Oathbreaker

Book 2: Shield of Winter

Book 3: Dawn of War

The Knights of Alana

Book 1: Daughter of Fate

Book 2: Queen of Vengeance

Book 3: Crown of Chaos

The Evolution Gene

Book 1: Reborn

Book 2: Havoc

Book 3: Carnage

Descendants of the Fall

Book 1: Warbringer

Book 2: Wrath of the Forgotten

Book 3: Age of Gods

Book 4: Dreams of Fury

The Alfurian Chronicles

Book 1: Defiant

Book 2: Guardian

Book 3: Conquest

The Swords of Heaven and Hell

Book 1: Darkstrider

The Four Circles

Book 1: Help! My Wizard Mentor Had A Heart Attack And Now I'm Being Chased By A Horde Of Giant Spiders!

The Untamed Isles

The Path Awakens